DOROTHY DIXON
SOLVES THE CONWAY CASE

DOROTHY DIXON

Solves the Conway Case

BY

Dorothy Wayne

Author of
Dorothy Dixon Wins Her Wings
Dorothy Dixon and The Mystery Plane
Dorothy Dixon and the Double Cousin

THE GOLDSMITH PUBLISHING COMPANY
CHICAGO

To
RUTH KIRBY
she says my books are "neat" . . .

CONTENTS

DOROTHY DIXON
SOLVES THE CONWAY CASE

Dorothy Dixon Solves the Conway Case

Chapter I

OUT OF LUCK

Above the speeding airplane, lowering black of approaching night and storm; below, the forest, grim and silent, swelling over ridges, dipping into valleys, crestless waves on a dark green ocean.

"We can't make it, Betty."

Dorothy Dixon, at the controls, spoke into the mouthpiece of her headphone set.

Betty Mayo, in the rear cockpit, glanced overside and shuddered.

"But you can't land on those trees!" she cried shrilly. "We'll crash—you know that!"

"Maybe we will—and maybe we won't!" returned Dorothy, gritting her teeth. "Keep your eyes peeled for a pond or a woodlot—anywhere you think we can land."

"What—what's the matter?" called back her friend, steadying her wobbly nerves with an effort.

"Matter enough. We're nearly out of gas—running on reserve fuel now. When the rain starts, it'll be pitch dark in no time."

"Oh, Dorothy—do try to stay up! We can't crash and be killed—that's what it will mean if you try to land here!"

"Betty, be-have, will you? This is my funeral." The pilot in her anxiety, had struck upon an unhappy choice of words.

"Oh, you must do something—this is ter-rible—" the frenzied girl in the rear cock-pit almost shrieked.

Dorothy ripped off her headphone set. She could no longer allow her attention to be distracted by Betty's excited whimper-ing.

The small amphibian, flying low, topped a crag-scarred ridge. At the foot of the cliff she saw a tiny woodland meadow.

Action in the air must be automatic. There is never time to reason. With the speed of legerdemain the young pilot sent her plane into a steep right bank and pushed down hard on the left rudder pedal. The result was a sideslip, the only maneuver by which the amphibian could possibly be piloted into the woodlot. Tilted sideways at an angle that brought a scream from terrified Betty, the heavy mass of wood and metal dropped like a plummet toward the earth.

This was too much for little Miss Mayo. Convinced that her friend had lost control of the plane, she closed her eyes and prayed.

With uncanny accuracy, considering the rainswept gloom, Dorothy recovered just at the proper instant. Hard down rudder brought the longitudinal axis of the plane into coincidence with its actual flight path again. At the same time she brought the up aileron into play, thereby preventing the bank from increasing. Then as the amphibian shot into a normal glide, she leveled the wings laterally by use of ailerons and rudder.

Their speed was still excessive, so for a split second or two, Dorothy leveled off and fishtailed the plane. That is, she kicked the rudder alternately right and left, thereby swinging the nose from side to side, and did so without banking and without dropping the nose to a steeper angle.

Taking the greatest possible care that her plane was in straight flight prior to the moment of contact with the ground, she gave it a brief burst of the engine, obviating any possibility of squashing on with excessive force. The airplane landed well back on the tail, rolled forward over the bumpy ground and came to a stop at the very edge of the little meadow, nose on to the line of trees and underbrush.

Dorothy switched off the ignition, snapped out of her safety belt and turned round.

"Hail, hail, the gang's all here," she said cheerfully. "Wake up, Betty! We've come to the end of the line."

Betty opened her eyes and looked about in startled amazement.

"Why—why we didn't crash, after all!"

"Certainly not," snorted Dorothy. "D'you think I'd let *Wispy* mash up my best friend? Come on, dry your eyes. Good thing it's so dark and none of the boys are with us. You'd be a fine sight," she teased.

"I think *Will-o-the-Wisp* is a silly name for a plane." Betty's remark was purposely irrelevant. She wanted to change the subject.

"Then don't think about it. Turn your mind upon the answer of that dear old song, 'Where do we go from here?'"

"Where are we?" Betty could be practical enough when her nerves were not tried too severely.

"Mmm!" murmured her friend. "That's the question. I'm not quite sure, but I think we're on the New York State Reservation over on Pound Ridge. A good ten miles or more from home, anyway."

"If we're on the reservation we're certainly out of luck," sighed Betty. "It's a terribly wild place—nothing but rocks and ridges and woods and things. They keep it that way on purpose."

"Nice for picnics on sunny days, I guess," affirmed Dorothy. "But not so good on a rainy night, eh? Here, put on this slicker before you're wet through. Then get down. We've got to move out of here."

Betty stood up, caught the coat Dorothy threw into the cockpit, and after slipping into it, she stared fearfully about.

"What are you waiting for?" Dorothy inquired from below.

"I'm going to stay where I am," announced Miss Mayo in a quavering voice. "It's safer."

"How safe?" Dorothy turned on her flash light. Its moving beam brought into bold relief the jungle of scrub oak and evergreens that walled the little pasture.

"Listen, Dorothy! I remember Father saying that they preserved game on the Pound Ridge reservation. There are sure to be bears and—and other things in these woods. Turn off the light—quick—they'll be attracted to us if we show a light—"

"Bears—your grandmother!" said Dorothy's mocking voice and the light flashed full on Betty. "Don't be so silly. Come down here at once!"

"No, I won't. I'm going to stay up here. I—I'm sure it's safer."

"Then you can be 'safer' by yourself. If you think I'm going to stick around this woodlot all night, you've got another guess coming. Snap out of it, won't you, Betty?"

"But you wouldn't leave me all alone out here!"

"Watch me." The light began to move away from the plane.

"I'll come—I'll come with you, Dorothy —wait!"

The light came back and Betty scrambled to the ground in a fever of haste.

"Now, then, stop being a goop and take this flash," directed Dorothy. "Hold it on the plane so I can see. We've got to make *Wispy* secure, before we get under way."

"I s'pose you get that Navy lingo from Bill Bolton." Betty felt rather peevish now. "You talk just like him ever since he taught you to fly."

"I wish he was here now," retorted her friend, and climbed into the cockpit. "Here—take these wheel blocks and stop grouching. And for goodness' sake, please don't wobble that light! I want to get these cockpit covers on before everything is flooded."

A few minutes later she climbed down again and after adjusting the wheel blocks, took the flashlight from Betty.

"All set?" she inquired briskly. "Got your knitting and everything? 'Cause it's time we were moving."

Betty began to cry.

"I think you're mean—of course I want to get out of here, but—but you n-needn't—"

Dorothy put her arm about the smaller girl's shoulders.

"There, there," she comforted, "cheer up. I won't be cross any more. Here's a hanky, use it and come along. Gee, I wish this rain would stop! It's coming down in bucketfuls."

"I'm sorry, too, for sniveling," said Betty meekly. She made a strenuous effort to be brave as they walked away from the dark shape of the plane. "But don't you think you'd better get out your revolver, Dorothy? Honestly, you know, we're likely to run into anything out here in these woods."

Dorothy burst into a peal of laughter. "Bless you, honey," she chuckled. "I don't carry a gun when I go calling—or any other time if I can help it. We'll get out of this all right, don't worry. I should have looked at the gas before we left home, but I thought there was plenty to take us over to Peekskill and back. *Wispy* eats the stuff—that's the answer!"

They stumbled along on the outskirts of the woodlot, Dorothy keeping her light swinging from side to side before them.

"But I thought you *always* carried a gun—" insisted Betty, her mind still on the same track—"you ought to, after all you went through with those bank robbers and then the gang of diamond smugglers!"

"Well, you've got to have a license to tote a revolver—I'll admit I've carried 'em now and then—but not to a tea!" replied her friend. "Do try and help me now, to find a way out of this place."

"But maybe there is no way out. We can't climb those cliffs, and this meadow's hemmed in by the woods. Oh, dear, I wish I knew where we are!"

"I'm not certain," mused Dorothy, more to herself than to her companion, "but I think I caught sight of the fire tower on the ridge just before we sideslipped. That would mean that this meadow is on the eastern edge of the reservation—and that there's a road on the hill across from the ridge. There must be a trail of some kind leading in here. They could never get the hay out or the cattle in, otherwise; this place must be used for something."

They trudged along, keeping the trees on their left until the farther end of the meadow was reached. As they rounded the corner the light from the flash brought into view a narrow opening in the trees and undergrowth.

"What did I tell you?" sang out Dorothy. "There's our trail! This certainly is a lucky break!"

"Where do you suppose it goes?" Betty's question was lacking in enthusiasm.

"Oh, it's the tunnel from the Grand Central to the new Waldorf-Astoria," said Dorothy, squinting in the darkness. "I'm going to take a room with a bath. You can have one, too, if you're good!"

Betty stumbled into a jagged wheel rut and sat down suddenly. "Oh, my goodness!" she moaned. "My new pumps are ruined—and these nice new stockings are a mass of runs from those nasty brambles!"

"Humph! Just think how lucky you are to be alive," suggested Dorothy callously. "Look—we're coming into another meadow. Yes—and there's a light— must be a house up there on the hill."

"What if they won't let us in?" wailed Betty.

They were heading across the meadow, now, toward the hill. Dorothy stopped and turned the flashlight on her friend.

"You certainly are a gloom!" she declared angrily. "Do you think I'm enjoying this? *My* shoes and stockings are ruined, too, and this ducky dress I'm crazy about has a rip in the skirt a yard long. It will probably be worse by the time we get through the brush on that hillside. But there's absolutely no use in whining about it—and there's not a darned thing to be scared of. Is that clear to you, Betty?" She paused, and then went on more gently. "Come on, old thing, you'll feel much better when we've found a place to get warm and dry."

"I know you think I'm an awful baby." Betty tried her best to make her voice sound cheerful, but her attempt was not a brilliant success. "But I'm just not brave, that's all," she went on, "and I do feel perfectly terrible."

"I know. You're not used to this kind of an outing, and I am, more or less. But I can see how it would upset you. Here's a stone fence. Give me your hand, I'll help you over. Fine! Now save your breath for the hill. We've got a stiff climb ahead of us."

For the next fifteen or twenty minutes they fought their way up the steep slope through a veritable jungle of thickets and rock. In spite of frequent rests on the boulders that dotted the hillside, both girls were exhausted by the time they came to another delapidated stone wall that acted as a low barrier between the brush and an over-grown apple orchard. Through the gnarled trunks, they could dimly see the shape of the house whence came the light.

Dorothy sat down on top of the wall, and pulled Betty to a place beside her. Then she switched off her flash.

"Some drag, that!" Her breath came in labored gasps.

Betty was too weary to make any reply. For a time they sat, silently. Then Dorothy slid painfully off the wall into the orchard.

"You stay here, Betty. I'm going over to the house and reconnoiter."

"Say! You don't go without me!" Betty sprang down with sudden determination.

"Then walk carefully and don't make any noise."

A tone of startled surprise came into Betty's voice.

"What—what are you afraid of, Dorothy?" she whispered excitedly.

"Not a thing, silly. But there may be

watch dogs—and I want to get some idea of the people who live in that dump before I ask 'em for hospitality. I've got myself into trouble before this, going it blind. I know it pays to be careful. If you must come with me, you must, I suppose. But walk behind me—and don't say another word."

She stalked off through the orchard with Betty close at her heels.

As they neared the house, which seemed to be badly in need of repair, it was plain that the light came from behind a shaded window on the ground floor. Dorothy stopped to ponder the situation. A shutter hanging by one hinge banged dully in the wind and a stream of rain water was shooting down over the window from a choked leader somewhere above. She felt a grip on her arm.

"Let's don't go in there," whispered Betty. "It's a perfectly horrid place, I think."

"It doesn't look specially cheerful," admitted Dorothy. "But there may not be another house within a couple of miles.

There's a porch around on the side. Maybe we can see into the room from there."

Together they moved cautiously through the rank grass and weeds to the edge of the low veranda. There was no railing and the glow from two long French windows gave evidence that the floor boards were warped and rotting. The howl of the wind and driving rain served to cover the sound of their movements as they tiptoed across the porch to the far window. Both shades were drawn, but this one lacked a few inches of reaching the floor.

Both girls lay flat on their stomachs and peered in. Quick as a flash, Dorothy clapped her hands over Betty's mouth, smothering her sudden shriek of terror.

Chapter II

TO THE RESCUE

The cold, wet wind of late September howled around the house. Dorothy wished she had brought a revolver.

"Stop it! Betty, stop!" she hissed and forced her friend to crawl backward over the rough boards to the edge of the porch. "Stay here, and don't make a sound. Do you want them out after us? For goodness' sake, take a grip on yourself! I'm going back to the window and—not another peep out of you while I'm gone!" With this warning, she slithered away before Betty could voice an objection.

Lying flat before the window once more with her face almost level with the floor, she stared into the room. The scene had not changed. Nor had the three principals of the drama being enacted on the other side of the pane moved from their positions. A sudden gust tore loose the shutter at the back of the house, sending it crashing down on some other wooden object with terrific racket.

"Must have hit the cellar doors," thought Dorothy.

The man with the cigar, who stood before the cold fireplace stopped talking. She saw him cock his head to one side and listen. The bald-headed man in the leather armchair kept his revolver levelled on the room's third occupant, and snapped out a question. With a shrug, the man by the fireplace went on speaking. He was a dapper person, flashily dressed in a black and white shepherd's plaid suit which contrasted disagreeably with the maroon overcoat worn open for comfort. Dorothy took a dislike to him at first sight. Not withstanding his mincing gestures, the man had the height and build of a heavyweight prizefighter. Now he leaned forward, emphasizing with a pudgy forefinger the point of his oratory which was directed toward the third member of the party.

Dorothy uttered an impatient exclamation. She could not hear a word. The roaring storm and the closed windows prevented her from catching even the rumble of their voices. She continued to gaze intently upon the prisoner, a well set up youth of eighteen or nineteen, curly-haired and intelligent looking. Her sympathy went out at once to this young fellow. He was bound hand and foot to the chair in which he sat. A blackened eye and his shirt, hanging in ribbons from his shoulders, told of a fight. Then she spied an overturned table, books and writing materials scattered over the rumpled rug.

"Whew!" she whistled softly. "He staged a little battle for 'em, anyway, I'll bet!"

She smiled as she noticed that the youth's opponents had likewise suffered. For the bald-headed man held a bloodstained handkerchief to his nose, while the other's overcoat was ripped from collar to hem and he nursed a jaw that was evidently tender.

The room which lay beneath her scrutiny offered a decided contrast to the unkempt exterior of the house. The walls were completely lined with bookcases, reaching from ceiling to floor. The shelves must have held thousands of volumes. Essentially a man's library, the furnishings were handsome, though they had evidently seen better days.

In reply to a question barked at him from the dapper prize fighter, the young prisoner shook his head in a determined negative. The big man spat out an invective. This time the boy smiled slightly, shook his head again. With a roar of fury that was audible to the watching girl outside, the prize fighter-bully strode over to his victim and struck him across the mouth.

That brutal action decided Dorothy. She wormed her way backward off the porch. Betty was still crouched where she had left her. She sprang up and caught her friend's arm.

"Isn't it terrible?" she whispered tensely. "He's such a good-looking boy, too—don't tell me they've killed him or anything?"

Without speaking, Dorothy led her around to the back of the house.

"No, they haven't killed him," she answered when they had reached the shelter of the apple orchard. "This is no movie thriller. But something pretty serious is going on in there. Now tell me—are you going to pull yourself together and be of some help? Because if you're not, you can climb one of these trees and stay there until it's all over. That's the only safe place I know of—and even up there you'll get into trouble if you start screaming again!"

"Well, I really couldn't help it, Dorothy. He was such a darling looking boy and—"

"My goodness—what have his looks got to do with it? He's in a peck of trouble—that's the principal thing. I want to help him."

"Oh, so do I!" asserted Betty eagerly. "I'll be good, honest I will."

"Obey orders?"

"Do my best."

"O.K. then. I'm going round front. Those blackguards must have come in a car—and I'm going to find it."

"But you can't leave me here alone—"

"There you go again, silly! I'm not

going to drive away in the car. I've got another plan. Listen! There's a cellar door, somewhere back of the house I guess. It's one of the flat kind that you pull up to open. I heard that shutter slam down on it."

"I suppose you want me to open it?"

"Bullseye!"

"You needn't be so superior," Betty's tone was aggrieved. "What'll I do if it's locked?"

"Oh, people 'way out in the country never lock their cellar doors," Dorothy's tone was impatient, her mind three jumps ahead.

"But suppose this one is?"

"Wait there until I come back. Hurry now—there's no telling what's going on in that room. So long—I'll be with you in a few minutes. If you hear a crash, *don't scream!*"

She raced away and as she reached the corner of the side porch, a quick glance over her shoulder told her that Betty was marching resolutely toward the cellar door.

This time Dorothy skirted the porch and toward the front of the house she came upon a weed-grown drive which swept in a quarter circle toward the road some fifty yards away. A limousine was parked before the entrance to the house. It was empty.

Dorothy breathed a sigh of relief. She hurried past the car and found that the drive ran round the farther side of the house, out to a small garage at the back. The garage doors were open, and inside she spied an ancient Ford. For some reason the sight of the Ford seemed to perturb her. She stood a while in deep thought.

Then as an idea struck home, she drew forth her flash light and sent its beam traveling over the interior of the garage. She did not take the precaution of closing the doors. The library was on the other side of the house and there was little danger of her light being seen. Suddenly she uttered a cry of satisfaction. Her light had brought into view about a dozen gasoline tins stacked in a corner. She lifted them one by one—all were empty. She hunted about and presently unearthed a short piece of rubber hose from under the seat of the automobile.

"First break tonight!" she said to herself. "Here's hoping the luck lasts!"

A few minutes later, if anyone had been watching, they would have seen a girl in a slicker, her dark curly hair topped by an aviation helmet, leave the garage carrying two gasoline tins. These she took to the orchard and deposited them behind a couple of apple trees.

Her next movements were more puzzling. She walked back to the garage and around that little building to the side away from the main house. Again her flash light was brought into play. This time she focussed it on the land to the side and rear and saw that the low wall which partly encompassed the orchard ended at the back of the garage. There was no obstruction between the drive at the side of the house and a rough field that sloped sharply down the valley whence she and Betty had come. Then she realized that the house and orchard lay on a plateau-like rise of land which jutted out into the valley from the main ridge, the ground dropping steeply on three sides.

"Well, the scenery couldn't be sweeter!" remarked Dorothy. "Now, I hope to goodness they've left the keys."

It was blowing half a gale now, and rain in crystal rods drove obliquely through the flash light's gleam. She switched off the light and stuffed it into a pocket of her dripping slicker and beat her way against the storm toward the house. Here she found the limousine, and hastened on toward the side porch.

Lying flat at the window once more, she saw that a fire had been started in the fireplace. The dapper person crouched before it, holding an iron poker between the burning logs.

Dorothy realized on the instant the fiendish torture those beasts were planning. She jumped to her feet and tiptoeing over the boards, raced for the car.

Her hand, fumbling on the dash, brought a faint jangle from a bunch of keys—

"Break number three!" she cried and slipped behind the steering wheel. As she switched on the ignition she brought her right foot down on the starter and when the powerful engine purred she fed it more gas and let in the clutch.

The car rolled forward and she swung it round the corner of the house toward the garage, with her thumb pressed down hard on the button of the horn.

"That'll bring them out!" she chuckled and slipping into high sent the car hurtling off the drive, headed for the field beyond the garage. An instant later she dropped off the running board while the limousine raced into the field and down the steep hillside to the valley below—and destruction.

At the same moment Dorothy heard shouts from the house and footsteps pounding on the gravel. She wasted no time peering after the car. Turning on her heel, she flew round the garage and over to the rear of the house. The cellar door was open, Betty was standing on the top step.

"Down you go!" panted Dorothy.

"Take this flash and switch on the light—quick!"

A slight shove sent Betty stumbling down the stone flight and Dorothy followed more slowly, bringing down the wide door over her head.

"The light, Betty, the light!" she cried.

"B-but we can't go into the house—those men—"

"Never mind the men—do as you're told. I can't find the lock on this door in the dark. Where are you, anyway?"

"Right here," said a small voice and the flash light gleamed.

Dorothy shot home the bolt and took the torch into her own hand.

"Come on!"

Without waiting to see if her order was obeyed, she ran to the stairs that led up to the first floor. At the top of the short flight, she found a closed door. She opened it and stepped into the kitchen, with Betty at her elbow. Locking the door behind them, she flashed her light about the room, then walked over to a table and pulled out the drawer.

"Here—take this!"

Betty stepped back as a large kitchen knife was thrust in her direction.

"Take it!" commanded Dorothy and again the smaller girl unwillingly did as she was told.

"But—but you can't mean we're going to fight them with knives," she spluttered, "why, Dorothy—I just couldn't—"

"Don't talk rot!" Dorothy's tone was caustic. "Please cut the argument, now— I know what I'm doing!"

Betty trotted at her heels as she crossed the kitchen toward the front of the house, passed through a swinging door into the dining room. An arched doorway to their right, brought the hall into view, and beyond it, another door stood open, leading into the lighted library, where they saw its single occupant still tied to his chair.

"Go in there and cut him loose," directed Dorothy.

She pushed Betty into the room and raced for the open front door. She heard the sound of voices from the drive as she neared the end of the hall. She could see the figures of two men just beyond the front steps. Just as her hand reached the door handle, they turned in her direction and the black night was seared with the sharp red flash from an automatic.

Chapter III

IN THE CONWAY HOUSE

With the detonation of the gun in her ears, Dorothy flung herself against the door and slammed it shut. Her hand fumbled for the key, found it and sent the bolt shooting into place. About the house the rain-lashed wind howled and moaned like some wild thing in torment. Her heart was pumping and her breath came in choking gasps. Leaning against the solid oak door she pressed her ear to a panel.

The noise of the storm muffled all other sound, but she thought she could detect the mumble of men's voices just outside the door. It was impossible to catch the words, of course, but the mere sound told the girl that they were standing on the small front porch. To her right was a sitting room. She hurried into it.

A quick flash of her torch showed two

windows facing the drive. She tried the
catches. They were unlocked. She fastened them and ran out of the room, down
the hall to the rear. The light from the
library threw the staircase into silhouette.
Dorothy started for the dining room, but
stopped short as the young man whom she
had sent Betty in to free, bounded into the
hall.

"Hello!" he cried. "Do you know where
they are?"

Dorothy pointed toward the front door.
"Right out there!"

"Good! I'll fix 'em!"

He raced up the stairs and she heard him
running toward the front of the house.

"Betty!" she called. "Come here!"

"What is it?" answered that young
lady's voice from the library. "George
told me to stay in this room."

"*George?*" exploded Dorothy. She ran
to the door and looked in. Betty was toast-
ing her soaking pumps from a chair before
the fire. She turned her head when Dorothy appeared and beckoned toward the
blaze.

"Yes—George Conway," she explained smilingly. "He owns this house, you see."

Dorothy's fingers pressed the wall switch and the electric lights went out.

"Well, you *are* a fast worker—" was her comment. "Dash over to those windows and see that they're fastened. Then pile some of these chairs and tables in front of the French doors—anything will do, just so it's heavy. Hurry—and when you've finished, go into the hall and stay there."

Betty stared through the darkness. "But George says—"

"I don't care *what* George says! The hall is the safest place right now."

"Well, why can't you help me?" grumbled Betty. "Suppose those awful men come before I've—"

"They won't if you snap to it. I'm off to fasten the windows in the rest of the house."

This last was thrown over her shoulder as she tore across to the dining room. After making the rounds in there she went into the kitchen. Here she found a window open and the back door unlocked. It took her but a moment to remedy this, and she was passing back to the dining room when there came a terrific crash and reverberation from the floor above, followed by screams and curses from outside.

She went out into the hall and another report from above shook the windows in their frames.

Betty, wild-eyed with fright, rushed into the bright arc of Dorothy's flash light.

"What on earth is it?" she cried in very evident alarm.

"Shotgun," said Dorothy tersely. "If those yells meant anything, I guess we can take it that somebody's been hit."

Then she noticed that Betty's left hand held an open compact, while in her right she clutched a small rouge puff. Her ash-gold hair which she wore long had become unknotted and hung halfway down her back. Her petite figure drooped with weariness.

"Gracious, Betty! How in the wide world did you ever get rouge on the end of your nose? You're a sight!"

"Well, you turned out the light—" Miss

Mayo's tone was indignant, as she rubbed
the end of her nose with a damp handkerchief. "I think I'll run upstairs and spruce
up a bit."

Dorothy looked at her and laughed.

"Come on up with me," suggested Betty.
"You don't look so hot yourself."

"No, you run along and pander to your
vanity, my child. When you've finished,
why don't you go into the kitchen and
make us a batch of fudge—that would be
just the thing!"

"Why so sarcastic?" Betty raised her
delicate eyebrows.

"Well—what do you think we've run
into—a college houseparty or something?"

"Oh, I think you're mean," Betty pouted.

"But you do choose the queerest times
to spiff up!"

"Do you think those men will try to get
in again!" Betty's blue eyes widened.

"If I didn't know that your head was
a fluffball—But what's the use. Run along
now. It sounds as if George were coming
down. Hurry up—you might meet him
on the stairs!"

"Cat!" said Betty and flew.

Dorothy went to the door and listened. If the two men were still outside, they gave no sign of their presence. Nothing came to her ears through the panels but the howl of the storm.

Then she heard footsteps running down the stairs from the second story and switched her flashlight on George. He carried a double barreled shotgun in the hollow of his arm.

"Howdy!" he greeted her enthusiastically. "You know, I can never thank you girls enough for all you've done. Gosh! You're a couple of heroes, all right—I mean heroines. When I saw Betty—I mean, Miss Mayo," he amended quickly with an embarrassed grin, "come sprinting into the library and begin to cut me loose, why I just couldn't believe my eyes!"

"Some wonderworker, isn't she?" Dorothy contrived to look awestruck, but there was no malice in her amused tone.

"You said it—she's a whizbang! And she told me you two came in an airplane. I've never met a girl aviator before. I guess she's a second Dorothy Dixon—you must have read what the newspapers said about that girl!" He shook his head admiringly. "Betty sure has nerve!"

"She has, indeed!" Dorothy kept her face straight with an effort. "But tell me—what did you do to that crew outside?"

"Plugged 'em—clean. Got a bead on them through a front window."

"What? You—killed them? Buckshot, at that distance?"

George chuckled. "Not buckshot—rock salt. Use it for crows, you know. It stings like the dickens."

"I'll bet it does!" Dorothy's laugh was full-throated and hearty.

"What's become of them?" she asked when she could speak.

"They beat it around the house to the garage. Do you know what happened to their car?"

"Yes. It ran away—down the lots to the bottom of the valley. And between you and me and the hatrack, I don't think it will ever run any more."

"Gee whiz!" chuckled George. "Who'd ever think a little thing like Betty would have the pluck to pull a stunt like that!"

"Who would?" said Dorothy and joined in the laugh.

"Well, as long as their car is out of the running, they'll probably try to steal my flivver." George tapped his gun significantly, "But I'll put a crimp in that. They've got to pass the dining room windows to get out of here."

"You needn't bother—the Ford won't move."

"Sure it will." George stopped short in the doorway and turned toward her. "That car of mine runs like a watch."

"But not without gas," explained Dorothy. "I drained the tank into a couple of tins."

"You did?"

"Sure thing. Parked the tins in your orchard. They'll never find 'em."

"Say!" exclaimed George. "You must be almost as good as Betty that is, I mean—"

"Who's taking my name in vain?" Miss

Mayo was tripping blithely downstairs. "You two seem to be finding a lot to talk about."

George stared at her. "Say, you certainly look swell when you're dolled up."

"Well, it's the best I can do now," deprecated Betty. "I borrowed a pair of your slippers though—woolly ones. That is, I s'pose they're yours?"

"Glad to have you wear 'em." George's eyes were still glued to Betty's pretty face when Dorothy broke in.

"Look here, we'll have to get down to business. George—listen to me. Betty won't melt, you know—"

"Oh, I think you're terrible—" interrupted Betty.

Her friend paid no attention, but kept on talking to George. "Do you really think they've gone?"

He nodded. "I'm pretty sure they have—that is, for the present. You can't do a whole lot when your hide is full of salt. I'll bet they're kiting down the road right now. Maybe they'll stop in at the Robinson's or somewhere and get a lift to Stamford or Ridgefield or wherever they came from. They may have some pals about here, of course. I sort of gathered that they weren't working on their own—that there was somebody in back of them."

"Well, at least we can count on a breather. Let's go in the library and turn on the light. I'm tired of standing about in this hall and I want to dry out by the fire."

In the library, George pushed a couple of easy chairs before the comforting blaze. Dorothy cast aside her slicker and helmet and dropped into one of them. She kicked off her sodden shoes and stretching her legs toward the warmth, drew forth a comb and proceeded to make herself neat. George perched on the arm of Betty's chair, and the two stared at the flames without speaking.

At last Dorothy put her comb away, turned to George and broke the silence.

"It's none of my particular business, of course, but would you mind telling me the reason for all this rough house? Why did those men attack you and tie you up—

what were they doing around here?"

George shook his head slowly. "Hanged if I know," he said.

"You don't know? But they seemed to be asking you questions—from what I could see through the window, it looked that way."

"That's right. But—but—well, you two girls are real sportsmen. You've pulled me out of an awful mess. Heaven knows I appreciate what you've done, but I just can't have you running any further risk on my account, Miss—"

"Dixon," supplied Betty. "I forgot you hadn't been introduced."

George leaned forward. "Do you come from New Canaan?" he shot out.

"Of course, we live there," said Betty. "And I want you to know that Dorothy is my best friend. We're seniors at the New Canaan High—if that interests you."

"So *you're* Dorothy Dixon, the flyer!" he exploded. "Suffering monkeys! I didn't know I was entertaining a celebrity. Why, you're the girl I was talking about—who—"

"Here, here—don't make me blush," laughed Dorothy.

"But don't you see? Your being Dorothy Dixon makes all the difference in the world."

Dorothy's eyebrows drew together in a puzzled frown.

"I don't get you," she said. "I really don't know what you're talking about."

"Why, if what the newspapers say is true, you simply eat up this gangster stuff—a whiz at solving all kinds of mysteries."

"Nice lady-like reputation, what?" she mocked.

"Well, that's all right with me. Because now—I have no hesitancy in telling you all I know about this queer business. You'll probably know just what to do—and you'll be a wonderful help."

"How about me?" Betty was a direct little person and seemed at no pains to disguise her feelings. "I don't think you're a bit polite, George!"

"Oh, I feel differently about you—" stammered that young man, then stopped short and looked painfully embarrassed.

Dorothy thought it time she took matters into her own hands.

"Don't be silly, Betty, George knows how clever you are!" She flashed a mischievous glance at her friend, then went on in a serious tone. "And of course we're keen to hear all about it, George, and we'll do anything we can to help you. But your story will keep a while longer. I hope you don't mind my mentioning such a prosaic thing—but do you happen to have anything to eat in the house?"

"Oh, my gosh! Of course I have—" he threw a glance at the clock and jumped to his feet. "It's nearly eight o'clock. You girls must be starved! Sit right here and I'll bring supper in a jiffy. I was just about to eat mine when those two thugs dropped in and put an end to it for the time being."

"I'll help you," offered Betty, hopping out of her chair.

"That's a good plan," decreed Dorothy. "While you're starting things in the kitchen, I'd like to use the phone, if I may."

"There it is, on that table in the corner," said George. "Hop to it. I'll drive you home later in the flivver."

"Thanks, but I've got to have gas for my plane. We'll talk it over at supper, shall we?"

She took up the telephone and the others hurried from the room.

Presently she joined them in the kitchen.

"I called up your mother, Betty, and told her you were spending the night with me," she announced. "Dad is away, so I got hold of Bill Bolton and he'll be over here in about twenty minutes."

"Oh, fine—" began Betty and stopped short as an electric bell on the wall buzzed sharply.

For a moment they stared at it in startled silence. Then George spoke. "Somebody's ringing the door bell," he said slowly.

Chapter IV

VISITORS

"You girls stay in here—I'll go," continued George, his hand on the swinging door to the dining room.

"No, you shan't!" Betty sprang before him, blocking his way.

"Don't make such a fuss," said Dorothy. "Somebody's got to go. Come here!"

Her long arm shot out and Betty was held in a light embrace that seemed as unbending as tempered steel.

"Stop wriggling," she commanded. "This is George's job. Did you leave your gun in the library, George?"

"Yes. I'll pick it up on the way."

"Better not do that. Maybe it's one of your neighbors."

"Haven't any. None of the people around here come to see me."

The bell buzzed loudly again, and continued to do so. Someone was keeping a finger pressed on the button beside the front door.

"I have a plan," Dorothy announced suddenly. "Betty, you stay here, and—"

"And have them break in the back door while you two are in the front hall? No thanks—I'm coming with you, that's all."

Dorothy did not stop to argue. She hurried into the dining room and across the hall to the library, followed by the others.

"Look here," she whispered, picking up the shotgun. "Slip on your jacket, George. That shirt will show anyone you've been in a fight. Betty and I will go into the front sitting room. It's dark in there. Turn on the hall light and open the door as though everything were all right, and you expected a friend. If it is someone you know, they won't see us in the sitting room. If it isn't—and they try to start something, jump back so you're out of line from the door to that room . . . and I'll fill 'em full of salt!"

"Swell idea! A regular flank attack!" enthused the young man, struggling into his coat. "All set?"

He switched on the hall light. The girls ran into the sitting room. Dorothy stood in the dark with the shotgun pointed toward the hall and saw him turn the key and pull open the door.

"Good evening, George," whined a high-pitched voice. "Mind if I come in for a minute or two?"

"Walk in, Mr. Lewis. Bad night, isn't it?"

George's face showed surprise but he swung the door wide and closed it with a bang as a tall figure, leaning heavily on a cane, shuffled into the lighted hallway. The man's bent back, rounded shoulders and the rather long white hair that hung from beneath the wide brim of his soft black hat, all bespoke advanced age. Immensely tall, even with his stoop, the old man towered over George, who was all of six feet himself. Although the night was not cold, he was buttoned to the chin in a long fur coat. Dorothy caught sight of piercing black eyes beneath tufted white eyebrows. The long, cadaverous, clean shaven face was a network of fine wrinkles.

"What say?" He cupped a hand behind his ear.

"I said it was a bad night to be out in," shouted George. "What can I do for you?"

"Yes, that's it, my lad—there's something I—Yes, it's a bad night—bad storm. Listen, George!"

"Yes, sir."

"What say?"

"I'm listening, Mr. Lewis."

"Well, listen then."

The sharp eyes peered up and down the hall. Dorothy moved further back into the dark room.

"Your father had a lot of books, George—a very fine library."

"Yes, he had."

"What say?"

"I said he had."

The old man shook his head. His high voice became querulous.

"I know he's dead," he snorted. "I'm talking about his books."

"They are not for sale," said George.

"Bless you—I don't want to buy 'em. But there's one I want to borrow."

"Which one is that?"

"What say?"

George's reply *sotto voce* was not polite. He was getting impatient.

"I want to borrow a book called Aircraft Power Plants; it's by a man named Jones."

Dorothy pricked up her ears.

"All right," shouted George. "I'll try to find it."

"What say? Listen, George! Speak distinctly, if you can. I'm not deaf—just a little hard of hearing. Don't mumble— you talk as though your mouth was full of hot potato. That's a bad eye you've got— been in a fight?"

George ignored this last. "Listen—" he said, then stopped, controlling a desire to giggle as he realized his plagiarism. "Come into the library, Mr. Lewis. I'll try to find the book for you." He took the old man by the arm and led him down the hall.

Betty crept over to Dorothy.

"Do you know who he is?" she asked in a low tone.

"Mr. Lewis, I gathered," said Dorothy, straining her ears to catch the muffled sounds coming from the library. "*He* talked loud enough,—quite an old gentleman, isn't he?"

"Old skinflint, you mean."

"You've seen him before?"

"Certainly. I've seen him at our house. Daddy knows him—says he's made a fortune, foreclosing mortgages and loaning money at high rates of interest. He's terribly rich, though you'd never know it by his looks."

"That's interesting—wonder what he wants with George?"

"Came to borrow a book—that's plain enough."

"Almost too plain, if you want my opinion," Dorothy said thoughtfully. "There's no use guessing at this stage of the game."

"What are you talking about?"

"Oh, nothing much. Can you hear what they're saying in the next room?"

"They seem to be having an argument— but it's not polite to listen—"

"Polite, your grandmother! I'd listen if I could—but all I get is a mumble-jumble. I vote we go back to the kitchen. I want my supper. I'll feel better when I've eaten. This house gives me the jim-jams for some reason."

"Me, too," Betty admitted ungrammatically. "Fancy being alarmed at the sound of a doorbell!"

"My word—and likewise cheerio!" Dorothy turned the flash on her friend. "How do you get that way, Betty? Been reading the British poets or something?"

Betty blinked in the glare. "Turn it off. No, I haven't. Don't you remember the movies last night? The English Duke in that picture—" She broke off suddenly and caught at Dorothy's arm. "Listen—Dot, listen!" she whispered.

From the rear of the house came a muffled pounding.

Dorothy shook her off. "I'll dot you a couple, if you take liberties with my name," she snapped. "And for goodness' sake, don't hold on to me that way, and stop that listen stuff! This isn't an earthquake—

somebody's at the back door, and I'm going to see who it is!"

"But suppose those men have come back?"

"They're too well salted down," Dorothy flung back at her. "I *fancy* you'd better stay in here—if you're *alarmed!*"

She crossed the hall to the dining room again and hurried through the kitchen with Betty close on her trail. That young person apparently preferred to chance it rather than be left alone.

Dorothy went at once to the back door.

"Who's there?" she called, as the knocking broke out again.

"It's Bill Bolton," returned a muffled voice. "Is that you, Dorothy?"

She drew back the bolt and flung the door open.

"Hello, Bill!" she hailed. "You're just in time for supper."

A tall, broadshouldered young fellow wearing golf trousers and an old blue sweater which sported a Navy "N" came into the room. He was bareheaded and his thick, close-cropped thatch of hair was brown. When he smiled, Bill Bolton was handsome. A famous ace and traveller at seventeen, this friend of Dorothy's had not been spoiled by notoriety. His keen gray eyes twinkled goodnaturedly as he spoke to Dorothy.

"Well, I should say you look pretty much at home," he grinned. "But then you have a faculty of landing on your feet. And how's Betty tonight? Thought I'd find you girls in a tight fix and here you are—getting up a banquet. Terry Walters was over at my house when you rang up, so he came with me. He's outside, playing second line defense. All sereno here, I take it?"

"Quiet enough now," Dorothy admitted, "though it was a bit hectic, to say the least, a while back. Call Terry in, will you? I'm going to do some scrambled eggs and bacon now."

She reached for a bowl and began to crack eggs and break them into it. Bill stuck his head out the door and whistled.

A moment later, a heavy set, round faced lad of sixteen made his appearance in the doorway. Under his arm he carried a repeating rifle.

"H'lo, everybody," he breezed, resting his rifle against the wall. "This is some surprise,—Bill and I were all set to play the heavy heroes and we find you making fudge!"

"Not fudge," corrected Betty. "Honest-to-goodness food! Dorothy and I haven't had a single thing to eat since lunch, except a lettuce sandwich and some cake at Helen Ritchie's tea over at Peekskill this afternoon. We're getting supper now."

"*We?*" Dorothy's tone was richly sarcastic. "Then, old dear, suppose you do some of the getting. I think I heard the front door shut just now, so that means that old Mr. Lewis has shoved off. You can go into the dining room and set the table.— Bill, you're a good cook—how about starting the coffee? Terry, be a sport and cut some bread—you might toast it while you're about it!"

"Whew!—some efficiency expert!" Terry winked at Bill. "Where do they keep the bread box in this house, anyway?"

"Barks her orders like a C.P.O. doesn't she?" laughed Bill, opening the coffee tin. Then he drew forth a wax-paper wrapped loaf from an enameled container, held it up: "Here's your bread, Terry—catch!"

The door from the dining room swung open and George came in.

"Well, George!" Dorothy turned to the others. "Here is our host," she explained and introduced him all round.

"It's certainly white of you fellows to hustle over here," he said as he shook hands. "I appreciate it."

"Oh, don't mention it," grinned Bill. "We seem to be rather late for the excitement."

"Well, if it hadn't been for Betty and Dorothy—" began George.

"You'd have pulled yourself out all right," interrupted the latter young lady. "Look here, supper's nearly ready, and since I've set everybody else to work, suppose I give you a job, too? Take Betty into the dining room and show her how to set the table, and you'll be a fine help."

"Say, it's great, the way you've pitched

in here—did you have a hard time finding things?"

"No, not at all. Except—" here Dorothy looked stern, "I don't approve of your housekeeping methods—I had to scour the frying pan twice, sir, do you realize that?"

George hung his head. "Gee, I guess I'm pretty careless, but—"

The cook giggled: "Mercy, you look downcast. I was only kidding, George. I think you're a fine housekeeper, honestly, I do. Now you get a wiggle on with the table, please. These eggs are nearly finished. They'll be ruined if we have to wait."

When the two had disappeared, Dorothy dished the scrambled eggs into a warm plate and turned to Bill and Terry.

"He thinks Betty ran this job," she informed them. "They've got a crush on each other, I guess. So don't put him wise, will you?"

"Mum's the word," smiled Bill, while Terry nodded. "Far be it from me to mess up love's young dream."

"Don't be silly," retorted Dorothy. "But

you know, Betty's a darling. I had to be terribly cross with her all the time, just to keep her bucked up. But she's my best friend and I'm crazy about her."

"She is nervous and high-strung, I know," supplemented Terry. "I'll bet you had a sweet time with her."

"Not so bad. Have you boys had supper?"

"Oh, yes, some time ago," answered Bill.

"That's good. I didn't want to use up all George's food. I'll let you have some coffee, though—that is, if you're good and don't kid those two in the other room."

" Cross-my-heart-hope-to-die-if-I-do . " Bill's face was solemn.

"Likewise me," declaimed Terry. "I must have my coffee."

"Table's set," announced Betty, popping in to the kitchen, closely followed by George.

"Eggs are finished and the bacon's fried," returned Dorothy. "How about the coffee, Bill?"

"Perfect—though I sez so."

"*And* the toast!" Terry was busy buttering the last slice. "You know, lovers used to write sonnets on their lady's eyebrows—now, if they'd seen this toast!"

Dorothy shook her head at him. "That will be about all from you. Come along, all of you—everything smells so good, and I'm simply ravenous."

It was a merry party that gathered about the old mahogany dining table. Bill began by teasing Dorothy about her lack of foresight that sent her up on a flight without enough gas. She returned his banter with interest: the others joined in and for a time everybody was wisecracking back and forth.

George was the first to bring the conversation back to current events.

"I don't know Mr. Lewis very well," he replied in answer to a question of Betty's. "He was a friend of my father's—at least father had business dealings with him. I thought I'd never get rid of the old boy tonight."

"Did you find the book he wanted?" asked Dorothy. "Jones' Aircraft Power Plants, wasn't it?"

"Some book, too!" affirmed Bill. "Have you read it, Conway?"

"Didn't know I owned it. The book—in fact, the whole library, was my father's. About all he saved from the wreck. When I couldn't find the book for old Lewis, what do you think he said?"

"'Listen!'" Dorothy's voice mimicked perfectly the old gentleman's querulous tones. Everyone burst into laughter.

"Yes, he said that," George told her, "and a whole lot more."

"I hate riddles," cried Betty. "Do tell us—"

"Why, he wanted to buy the entire library—and when I turned him down, he made me an offer on the house providing entire contents went with it!"

Betty laughed. "A good low price, I'll bet. Mr. Lewis is a terrible old skinflint."

"I thought so, too, until he made me this offer."

"Do you mind saying how much?" Dorothy never hesitated to come to the point.

"Twenty-five thousand dollars!"

"Seems like a lot of money to me!" was Bill's comment.

"A lot of money! I should say so." George cried excitedly. "Why, this place isn't worth more than eight—possibly ten thousand dollars at the outside."

"I smell a rat," said Terry, "or to put it more politely, the old boy's offer has something doggoned stinking crooked mixed up in it."

"To add to our cultured brother's oratory," said Bill, "There certainly seems to be something pretty darned putrid in the kingdom of Denmark!"

"A whole lot nearer home, if you ask me," broke in Dorothy.—"That old man—"

"Just a moment," begged Bill. "Your deductions, Miss Dixon, are always noteworthy. In fact, at times, the press of our glorious country has frequently referred to you as Miss Sherlock Holmes, but—"

"Cut the comedy, Bill!" broke in the object of this effusion. "What is it you're driving at?"

"Simply, as I was saying when so rudely

interrupted, that your deductions and ideas on this business may be A1 and a yard wide, but except for what you shot at me over the telephone, both Terry and I are wading about in a thick pea soup fog, so to speak. Suppose you give us your account of these mysterious happenings. That should put us 'hep' to the situation, and then George can tell us his end of the story, why he got tied up by these blokes and all that."

George did not appear cheerful. "But I don't know—" he protested. "Haven't the slightest idea."

"So Dorothy said over the phone. But perhaps if you start far enough back— give us the story of your life, as it were— we may be able to dig out a motive."

"At times you show positively human intelligence, Bill!" Dorothy yawned, without apology. "Well, here goes! Maybe if Bill will let me get a few words in edgewise, I may forget I'm so sleepy!"

Chapter V

THE MOTIVE

"And then I opened the back door and found you standing there, Bill. Phew!" Dorothy ended with a sigh. "It's almost more of an effort in the telling than it was in the doing!"

"I wouldn't believe it if I didn't know it was true," declared Terry solemnly.

"You've the great gift of stating things clearly, Terry," remarked Bill Bolton. "In other words, why must you put in your foot every time you open your mouth? Dorothy, my girl, you said your piece nicely."

"I'm not your girl, thank heaven! If I was at all interested, I'd certainly burst into tears. Please don't try to be humorous—it's painful, positively painful."

"I guess I'd better begin my story," George decided diplomatically. "Or somebody's likely to start throwing things. Where do you want me to start?"

"Like this," volunteered Terry, setting his empty coffee cup on its saucer. "'I was born an orphan at the age of four, of poor but dishonest parents. . .'"

"'And until the age of thirteen and three-quarters, could only walk sideways with my hair parted in the middle,'" came George's quick follow up.

"He's all right," decreed Bill. "Let him speak his piece, gang—this is going to be good."

"Of all the conceited nerve!" exclaimed Dorothy.

"Do shut up and give George a chance," broke in Betty heatedly. "I want to hear about it—and this is a serious matter, I—"

"Now you're the one who's stopping him," accused her chum. "For goodness' sake, get going, George—we've got to drive to New Canaan some time tonight."

"All right," said George. "If you people don't find it interesting, well, you've brought it on yourselves. Surprising as it may seem, I was born at the usual age at 'Hilltop,' that big whitehouse on the ridge, overlooking the other side of the reservation. Father, you know, was an inventor. He was always an extremely reticent man and I realized as I grew older that he was very much of a recluse. He never spoke to Mother and me about his inventions, but they must have brought him a good income. We kept up that big place and had plenty of servants, although we entertained very little. After I got through the nursery stage, I had a French governess and later a tutor. Mother and I were great pals. She must have been a busy woman, for she superintended the running of our model farm and dairy, but she was never too occupied with her duties but what she had time to romp and play with me. I know now that she must have led a very lonely life.

"My father spent nine-tenths of the time in his laboratory and workshop. He did not encourage friends or acquaintances and he never went anywhere with Mother. He had but one hobby, his work, and although I know he was very fond of us, the work came first. Even later, when I grew up, he never seemed like the fathers of other fellows I knew. It was his reticence and absolute absorption in those inventions of his that kept us practically strangers.

"Five years ago last spring, when I was twelve, Mother died. Her heart had never been strong—her going took the only person I really loved away from me."

George was unable to go on for a moment, and Betty caught his hand under the table and held it. The tenderhearted little girl was very near to tears. George smiled manfully, then went on with his recital.

"Sorry," he apologized for his show of feeling, "I never quite got over losing Mother. My governess had been replaced by a tutor a couple of years before this, but now Father decided I was to go to boarding school. So I was packed off to Lawrenceville, a homesick, lonely little kid if there ever was one. I'd never been thrown with boys of my own age before—I guess I was pretty much of a young prig—but as the poet says, 'I soon learned different.'

"During the holidays I used mostly to come back to Hilltop. Father never made a kick if I brought fellows back with me.

We had the run of the place, which he kept up just as it had been when Mother was alive. One thing was understood though: he must not be annoyed by my guests. There were saddle horses, for he rode regularly every morning before breakfast; cars to drive, and he also belonged to the club over at Bedford, although I don't think he had ever seen the place. He gave me plenty of money to spend and always allowed me to accept invitations from other fellows to visit at their homes. Altogether I had a pretty good time. The only trouble was that Father never took any real interest in me. I was lucky enough to get my "L" at football, but he never came down to Lawrenceville—not even to see a game."

"I've got your number, now!" cried Terry, interrupting him. "You're Stoker Conway! I thought I'd seen you before. Say, Bill, this guy is too modest. 'Lucky to make his letter,' I don't think! Conway captained the Lawrenceville team last season. My cousin, Ed Durham (they call him Bull Durham down there) played left tackle. I went down with Dad and Uncle Harry last fall to see the Princeton freshman-Lawrenceville game."

"I remember your telling about it," said Dorothy. "Somebody, I think, made a sixty-yard run for a touchdown."

"I'll bet George did it," piped up Betty.

"He certainly did! And let me tell you, Angelface, that your boy friend was the fastest halfback Lawrenceville or any other school has seen in years. All American stuff—that's what he is. Hard luck you didn't get to college this year, old man."

"Can't always have what we want," remarked George philosophically.

"Who won the game?" asked Bill. "The one you saw, Terry?"

"Why, Lawrenceville, of course. Smeared 'em—outplayed those freshies from start to finish and did it with a lighter team. Thirty-three to nothing—think of it!"

Dorothy turned toward George.

"Stoker Conway—I like that name, 'Stoker.' How did you get it?"

George grinned. "I was a grubby little mutt—my first term at Lawrenceville. Somebody pasted the name on me, and it stuck."

"Three celebrities at one table," sighed Terry. "I knew we had two with us to-night—but a third! It's just too much. Betty, you and I have just got to do something to make ourselves famous. There's practically no hope for me, I admit, but you will probably become a movie queen, when you're old enough,—ash-gold hair and a baby doll face are all the rage on the screen!"

"Oh, I don't know," hit back Betty, ignoring the laughter caused by this left handed compliment. "How about the fame you won in the diamond smuggling case? You got plenty of newspaper publicity then."

This sally turned the laugh on Terry, for as the three others knew, he had played anything but an heroic part in that episode.

But Terry was a jolly soul and his hearty laugh at his own expense joined with the others.

"Lay off, Betty!" he cried, "that was one below the belt. What do you bet I spot the motive in this mysterious case of Stoker's?"

"See here, will you pipe down?" Bill expostulated. "All you will spot is your clothes. Keep quiet and quit waving your arms—you nearly upset my coffee. How can any of us learn anything unless you give Stoker a chance to get on with his story?"

Terry suppressed a retort and George hurried into the breach.

"Here goes on the second installment, then," he said. "And it will probably interest you all to know I'm pretty near the end. Let's see—where was I?"

"Last fall, at Lawrenceville," prompted Dorothy. "You couldn't get your father to come down there."

George nodded. "Yes, that's right. He never would come—not even when I graduated last June. I wrote him specially about it, but, well, he was having his own troubles about that time. Before I came home I passed my finals for Princeton. It was on the books that I'd go there this fall.

"Only I didn't," continued young Conway rather solemnly. "Father met me at the Bedford station in the flivver when I came back. On the way up here he told me that reverses in business had forced him to sell Hilltop. I knew, of course, that business conditions were pretty bad all over the country. But he looked ill and he had aged terribly since I'd seen him during the Easter holidays. I was much more worried about his physical condition, he seemed so played out, so feeble. But when we drove into the yard and I saw this down-at-the-heels old house—well, I certainly got another shock."

"It must have been terribly hard," sympathized Betty. "Especially after living all your life in the big place on the hill."

"A bit of a comedown," acknowledged George, "but I don't want any of you to think I was ashamed of the place. If Father had to live here, it was good enough for me. I felt so sorry for him, though. He'd never been much of a mixer, as I said, but when he did talk to a fellow he was certainly interesting, full of pep and vitality—and a sure hog for work. Now all that was changed. He had no workshop or laboratory here. All day long and half the night he would sit reading in the library across the hall. If I spoke to him, he would answer 'yes' or 'no' to a question—but never volunteered anything on his own account. He seemed more like a man stunned—a man who realizes his life is a failure and no longer cares to go on.

"The woman down the road who cooks and keeps the house clean told me he had moved in here the early part of April and that during the time before I came back, he had been exactly as I found him.

"I wanted to get a job in the city. Even though I couldn't get him to talk about his affairs, I knew he couldn't have very much money, living in a ramshackle place like this. But though I wanted to get out and earn some money, I realized I must stay with him for the time being—and I'm glad I did. Father passed away in his sleep the night of July fourth. The doctor said it was his heart—like Mother.

"Well, I guess that's about all of it. When the will was read I found that he'd left me everything. It amounted to two thousand dollars in cash, and this house and the sixteen acres that go with it. I stuck on here for the rest of the summer, trying to get the place in better shape; gave the house a couple of coats of paint, reshingled parts of the roof, and have done as much as I could. I'm trying to sell the place, you know, and the agent told me I could never do it unless it was put in better condition. It looks pretty bad still, but I've worked like a dog.

"And I forgot to say, that Mr. Lewis bought Hilltop from father. He drops in here every once in a while for a chat. I know he's got a reputation for being a skinflint, but I sort of like the old man, anyway."

Dorothy, who had been absent-mindedly rolling bread pills on the table cloth, threw him a sharp glance.

"What happened tonight, before we came?" she asked.

"Why, I was just about to get my supper,

when the bell rang. I opened the door and those two guys jumped me."

"Not very subtle, were they? What do you suppose they were after?" Bill looked inquiringly at George.

"Well, this is the funny part of it all. They said they'd come for the letter Father had left for me to read after his death—"

"And you didn't give it to them?"

"I'd never even heard of such a letter. I told them so."

"And they wouldn't believe you, eh?"

"They thought I was bluffing, of course."

"But how on earth—did they say anything about the contents of the letter?" This question came from Dorothy.

"No. Simply that they wanted it—and they knew I must have it. What I can't understand is how they could be so sure that a letter exists—even if I'd known about it, I wouldn't have given it to them—but it's all as clear as mud to me."

"Has Mr. Lewis ever spoken to you about it?"

"Never."

"Have you any reason to suppose that your Father might have left a letter for you—any idea that he might have had an important message to convey to you in that way?"

"Not the slightest. You see, I—"

"Look here," broke in Terry. "Do you think it possible that old Lewis knew that your Father wrote you that letter—and believes that it's in this house? He might have hired those thugs to get it from you, then when he found out they failed, he hopped over here himself and made that offer to buy your place, in order to get hold of it? There may be something valuable contained in it, and he wants to get it at any cost."

"Too crude," declared Dorothy with a shake of her head. "Perhaps he does want to buy it—but I doubt if he has anything to do with those holdup fellows. Mr. Lewis may be close but I'm sure he's a clever man. The very fact that he came here so soon after the fracas clears his skirts of trying to hold up Stoker. As I say, he may want to get hold of the letter himself, but I'm

dead sure he's not the nigger in this particular woodpile."

"Then who is?" Terry wanted to know.

"Tell us that, and you'll win the fame
you're after," chuckled Betty.

"Just a moment," Bill was speaking
again. "If old Lewis is as clever as you
think he is, Dorothy, then the smart thing
for him to do would be exactly what he *has*
done!"

"How's that?"

"Well, if he did hire those lads, he might
figure that by coming over here, Stoker'd
begin to believe he was the man behind the
gun. *But,* he might have realized that on
second thought, Stoker would discount the
idea, for the very reason you have done
so."

"Gosh!" exploded Terry. "That's a
stumper, Bill. What are we going to do
about it?"

"That's the question—*can* we do anything?" Dorothy flicked a bread pill
across the table.

Chapter VI

CORNERED

"There's one thing about it," Bill Bolton told the others seated at the supper table. "This letter that Mr. Conway is supposed to have written to Stoker is at the bottom of all this queer business."

"But that doesn't get us anywhere, does it?" objected Terry. "We must find out what that letter's about. Get hold of the underlying motive, you know."

"Say, you got that out of a detective story—'underlying motive'—I know you did." Betty shook an accusing finger at him.

"Well, what of it? That's the thing we've got to do—and I guess it doesn't matter how you say it."

"Enter Doctor Watson!" Bill grinned and winked at Dorothy. "Look out for your laurels, Miss Sherlock Holmes!"

"Oh, come on—this isn't any jazz num-

ber," she returned with spirit. "What's
your big idea, Terry?"

"Why, hunt for the letter of course.
When we find it, we'll have the—ahem!—
underlying motive as well."

"Maybe. Who's going to do the hunting?"

"All of us. We'll each take a room,
and—"

Dorothy laughed. "You're some organ-
izer. Suppose you start in with the library.
It won't take you more than a week to go
through all the books in that room!"

"But listen, Dorothy—"

"Don't be absurd. We'll have a hunt
tomorrow, if you want. But Betty and I
have got to get home now—and anyway, I
know where that letter is."

The four about the table stared at her
in unfeigned amazement.

"*Where?*" they cried in chorus.

"I'll give each of you three guesses," she
went on mischievously.

"Oh, don't be horrid," pleaded Betty.

"You know we're absolutely up a
tree—" chimed in George.

"Come on and tell," invited Bill.

"How did you find out?" added Terry.

"Simply by keeping my eyes and ears open," retorted the object of this wordy bombardment, "and by knowing that two and two make four, not sometimes, but all the time. Every one of you has heard as much about this as I have tonight, and every one, excepting Stoker, has kidded me because I found out some things about the bank robbery and that smuggling gang this summer. Now you won't even take the trouble to think for yourselves. The whereabouts of that letter is clear enough; to be able to put our hands on it, is something quite different."

"Well, I apologize for us all," Bill leaned across the table, "we were only kidding you—weren't we, Betty?"

"Why, of course—she knows that, she's only trying to—"

"Come on, Dorothy," Terry coaxed her with a grin.

"The letter is—?" George asked soberly.

Dorothy pursed her lips, then smiled.

"In your father's copy of Jones' Aircraft Power Plants," she replied calmly. "Find that book, which Mr. Lewis was so keen to locate that he offered to buy this house in order to get it—and you'll have the letter."

"I believe you're right," conceded Bill, "you generally are—but that book is going to take some finding, or I've got another guess coming."

"If there really is a letter and it's in the book," said George, "Mr. Lewis must have hired those men."

"Not necessarily," returned Dorothy, "but I'll admit it's possible."

George's face wore a puzzled frown. "What I can't understand is why outsiders should know about this letter, when I have never heard of it."

"And if your father really wrote a letter to you, and they knew it—why did they wait nearly three months before they tried to steal it?" Bill shook his head. "It's beyond me."

"And why did they start in using strong arm stuff right off the bat?" Terry propounded this question to the table at large.

"Well, I think it is the most mysterious thing I ever heard of," said Betty, struggling to stifle a yawn.

Dorothy stood up.

"Well, we can't talk about it any longer tonight. Betty and I must be getting home." She turned to Bill. "Did you bring some extra gas for *Wispy?*" she asked. "From the sound of things outside, the storm seems to be pretty well over. I don't want to leave the plane in that woodlot all night. Some tramp might come across her and bust something."

"I've brought enough gas to fly back to New Canaan and then some. I'll go with you in the plane."

"How about me?" Betty looked surprised, yet oddly hopeful.

"Terry'll drive you home," said Bill.

George looked disappointed, but voiced no objection to the plan, and Betty merely shrugged.

Dorothy spoke up quickly. "No, I think you'd better stay here tonight, Terry. Somebody ought to stay here with George . . . pardon me, Stoker! But as it's Sunday tomorrow, there's no school to get up early for, and Stoker can drive Betty over to my house and come back here. Bill and I will bring her over after breakfast and we can see what we can do to locate that letter."

"Good plan," agreed young Conway enthusiastically. "I'll be back in less than an hour."

"But who's going to wash all these dishes?" grumbled Terry.

"Not afraid to stay here, are you?" said Dorothy.

"Oh, if you put it that way I'll wash them," he retorted.

"You do 'em tonight, and we'll do 'em tomorrow—but we really must be going now."

Ten minutes later, Betty and George chugged out of the drive in his flivver. Terry parked Bill's car in back of the house, then he helped his friend to lift out the three large tins of gasoline they had brought with them from New Canaan.

"I'll take two," announced Bill, "and you'll have to tote the other one, Dorothy."

"Hadn't I better carry it down the hill?"

suggested Terry. "It's kind of heavy."

"No, thanks, I can manage it all right." She lifted the can by its handle. "It's not so heavy. Your job is to stay in the house. As it is, I hate leaving you here alone."

Terry waved them off.

"I'll be all right," he scoffed. "I think we've got those guys buffaloed—for the time being, anyway."

"Keep your rifle handy," advised Bill, "and don't open up to anyone except Stoker."

"You bet I won't."

"Good night, then—"

"And good luck," added Dorothy, switching on her flash.

"Good night, both of you—see you in the morning."

He watched their light travel into the orchard and turned back to the empty house.

Dorothy and Bill reached the rear wall of the orchard and came to a stop. Although the storm had passed and with it the driving rain, heavy cloud formations obscured the stars.

"Better hop over the fence, Dorothy," said Bill, "then I'll pass these containers across to you. Gee whiz! It sure is some black night. You came up this way, didn't you?"

"Yep." Dorothy's voice came from the other side where her light was flashing. "Hand over the cans. That's right."

Bill joined her and picked up his load again.

"The ground slopes down to the valley from here," she said. "Drops would be a better word, I guess. It goes down like the side of a roof. Watch your step! This wet grass is slippery as ice."

"I've found that out," said Bill, sitting down suddenly. "Which way is that woodlot trail from here?" He got to his feet. The tins had saved him from a bad tumble.

"Off to the right—down in the valley."

"Then let's steer off that way. Take this hill on the oblique. It's easier walking. By the way, which side of the river have you got the bus parked?"

"River? What river? I didn't know there was one."

"Well, there is.   Stone Hill River, it's called.   If you didn't cross it going up to Stoker's house, the plane must be on this side."

"You've got a master mind," she retorted and her light went out.

"What's the matter?"

"Followed your example, and sat down."

The light flashed on again.

"Aren't hurt, are you?"

"Don't be personal," she laughed. "How did you know there was a river down in the valley?"

"Why, I brought a map of the Reservation with me—studied it on the way over while Terry drove.   We'd never have found that dirt road Stoker's house is on otherwise.   Part of it is really in the Reservation, you see.   The concrete road from Poundridge Village that runs to South Salem parallels it about a quarter of a mile to the east."

"Route 124," said Dorothy, walking carefully for fear of slipping again.   "I know that road.   Ever been in the Reservation, Bill?"

"No—have you?"

"When I was a little girl, we used to drive over, for picnics sometimes. I don't remember much about it, though, except that it's a terribly wild place—all rocks and ridges and forest. It covers miles. The state has cut trails and keeps them open, otherwise the woods have been left in their virgin state."

"There are cabins, too, the map calls them shelters," Bill informed her. "The state rents them to camping parties. Well, it's quite wild enough to suit me right here. How are you making out?"

Dorothy was leading the way with her light.

"Fine, thanks. I'm on the level again."

"Glad to hear that you are," chuckled Bill.

"Silly! I mean I'm on fairly level ground again. And look what I've found."

Her light flashed to the left and came to rest on the wreck of a seven passenger closed car.

"Good enough!" exclaimed Bill. "Those thugs won't do any more riding in that bus.

See how the car smashed that big tree—it must have torn down the hill like greased lightning!"

They deposited their gasoline tins on the grass and inspected the mass of twisted metal more closely.

"Hello!" ejaculated Dorothy. "Someone's been here before us."

"How do you figure that?"

"The license plates have been removed. I know they were on the car when I sent it down here. I was in such a rush I forgot to take the number, worse luck!"

"Too bad—now we won't be able to trace the owner."

"Oh, yes, we will. Unless we've got an unusually clever mind bucking us, I'll bet we can trace it through the factory number and the number of the engine. Give me a hand, Bill. Let's get the hood up."

"Master mind number two," grunted Bill when Dorothy's flash was turned on the motor. "Him and me both, eh? The number plate has been removed, and the one on the engine chiseled off. Those lads must have had a lovely time doing it, with their hides full of salt."

Dorothy switched off her light with a click.

"*They* never came down here, in their condition," she said decisively. "It must have been somebody else—probably the man who is back of them—or others of that gang."

"Old Lewis?"

"I don't know. Of course, he himself couldn't have done this—"

"Yes, he's a bit too old to come traipsing down to this valley all alone in the dark."

"Too bad we've showed our light on the hill and around here just now," she said slowly.

"You think they may still be in the offing?"

"I hope not. Chances are they don't know about the plane."

"You'd better go back to the house," he advised. "I can lash two of these tins together and sling them over my shoulder. If there's going to be a shindy, you'll be better off up the hill with Terry."

"Thanks a lot," said Dorothy. "If there's going to be trouble, we'll go it to-gether. Anyway, you'd never be able to find the trail to the woodlot in the dark. It's great of you to suggest carrying on without me, but it just can't be done."

"You sure are a good sport, Dorothy." Bill picked up his tins. "Where do we go from here?"

"Follow me. And the less noise we make, the better."

With Bill close on her heels, she led across the clearing toward the dark line of trees on their left, winding her way around rocky out-croppings and stunted bushes that made traveling in the dark a difficult proceeding.

"Think you can find the cart road?" she heard him whisper. "It's black as your hat without the flash."

"Sure can," she replied cheerfully. "All we have to do is to turn right at the woods and follow them up the valley until we come to it. Quiet, now—if anybody's watching, we may be able to get by them in the dark."

They had gone another twenty yards or so, when Dorothy stopped suddenly and caught at Bill's arm.

"There's somebody behind that big rock to the left!" she whispered fiercely. "I'm sure I saw something move."

"You sure did, young lady," announced a gruff voice close to their right. "Tell your girl friend not to make a fuss, Mr. Conway. My men are all around you."

A tall figure, hardly more than a blur in the darkness, stepped from behind a tree and came toward them.

Chapter VII

RAVEN ROCKS

Bill Bolton dropped one of the gasoline tins he was carrying and grasping the other with both hands, hurled its heavy bulk at the stranger. The tin caught the man full in the chest.

As he staggered back, Dorothy felt herself seized from behind. A quick twist and pull sent her antagonist hurtling off to the right. It was not for nothing she had put in long hours mastering the complicated throws and holds of jiu jitsu, that strenuous art of Japanese wrestling.

She freed herself in time to see Bill crash his fist into the face of a third man.

"Come on!" he yelled, and they raced for the line of trees.

But their troubles were not over yet. Straight ahead and directly in their path, another dark figure was leaping toward them. There was no time to dodge—to swerve. Bill dove at the man, stopping him short and bringing him to the ground with a clean tackle just above his knees. The force of contact was terrific. For the fraction of a second neither the tackler nor his opponent moved. Then as Dorothy, trembling with excitement, bent over them, Bill scrambled to his feet.

"Are you hurt, Bill?" The girl's voice was breathless with concern.

"No—only winded—" he gasped. "Be all right—in a minute."

Dorothy gripped him by the arm and they trotted forward again, gradually increasing their speed as Bill regained his breath. From behind them came the calls and angry shouts of their pursuers.

All at once, the inky black blur of the woods loomed before them.

"Keep along the edge of this pasture toward the wood road," Dorothy whispered quickly. "I'm going to start a false trail. Maybe we can fool them. You get your breath—join you in a minute or two."

She sprang into the underbrush, crashing over low bushes, snapping dead twigs and branches under foot with all the clatter of a terrified cow in a cane brake. Then the noise stopped as suddenly as it started, and Bill was surprised to hear her light footsteps at his heels.

"I want 'em to think we're hiding in there," she explained hurriedly. "Can you run now?"

"You bet!"

They sped along the edge of the wood, spurred by the thought that the ruse would delay their pursuers and perhaps throw them off the trail altogether. From their rear came the sound of a rough voice issuing commands. Men were beating the underbrush, cursing in the darkness.

Both Dorothy and Bill had got their second wind and were running much more easily now. Then Dorothy tripped on the uneven ground and would have fallen had not Bill thrust out a steadying hand.

"Thanks," she said jerkily as she ran. "Look over my shoulder. Lights back there."

"Wonder they didn't use 'em before," was Bill's only comment.

Dorothy slowed down to a fast walk and Bill also slackened his pace.

"We must be nearly there," she panted, "though since we had to drop the gasoline, there doesn't seem much use hiking over to the plane."

Bill nodded in the darkness. "Think we'd better get back to the house?"

"Yes; they'll never see us, especially now that they've got their flashlights going— that glare will blind them. I vote we keep on along the valley until we pass the wood road, then swing across this pasture again and up the hill till we strike the road. That will take us back to the Conway place and—

"Look!" Bill's exclamation arrested her, but his warning was unnecessary. Far above, a sudden rift in the clouds brought a full moon into view. The woods, the open pasture and the steep hill down which they had traveled almost blindly a few minutes before were now bathed in clear, silvery light as bright as day. As they dashed forward again, a shout from behind told them they had been seen.

"Stop or we'll fire!"

"There's the trail, Bill—it's our only chance!"

Men were calling to each other behind them and she caught the sound of heavy feet pounding along in their wake. As she and Bill turned into the wood road and sped down its winding stretches under the arch of intertwining boughs, a revolver cracked several times in quick succession. Overhead, the bullets went screaming through the branches.

"Shooting high to scare us," wheezed Bill. "'Fraid we're running into a dead end."

"Maybe not—this moonlight won't last —clouds too heavy."

Dorothy wasted no more breath in speech. Her every effort was centered in keeping up with the long legged young fellow who seemed to cover the ground so easily and at such an amazing rate of speed.

Presently they swept out of the wagon-trail and into the glaring moonlight of the woodlot. Shouts and calls from their pursuers but a short distance behind now, lent wings to their feet. At the far end of the open space, Dorothy's amphibian lay parked where she had left it.

"Not that way!" warned Bill and caught her arm as she started to swing toward the airplane. "Straight ahead!"

There was no time for argument. Dorothy swerved and dashed across the lot, following his lead. Straight ahead lay a narrow belt of woods which ended abruptly in precipitous cliffs towering upward almost perpendicularly for several hundred feet to the top of the ridge. What Bill's plan might be, she could not guess. Those sheer palisades certainly could not be scaled. What could his objective be? If they turned up or down the valley the enemy would be sure to hear them tracking through the thick underbrush. And there would be no chance of outflanking the pursuit, for the men were between them and the Conway house.

She and Bill were trapped at last— trapped by walls of rock and the encompassing ring of the enemy.

They reached the farther edge of the field

where a hurried glance behind showed them that the men were plunging out of the wood road. Then the moon, perhaps ashamed of the trouble he had brought them, swam away behind another cloud formation, and once again the world was sunk in darkness.

Bill's fingers gripped her hand.

"Follow me. Walk carefully and hold your arm before your face. It's a case of feel our way till we get used to the gloom— and there's no sense in losing an eye."

He led onward through the wood and although Dorothy could see nothing but an opaque blackness before her eyes, Bill never hesitated in his stride. With his hand behind his back, he pulled her forward as though guided by an uncanny knowledge of invisible obstructions in their path.

"How do you do it?" she marveled. "Don't tell me you can actually see to dodge these branches and tree trunks?"

She heard him chuckle.

"Not *see*—feel. I learned the trick in the Florida swamps last summer. Osceola, chief of the Seminoles, taught me."

"Oh, yes! He's a wonder in the woods. How is it done?"

"Tell you sometime. Here we are—at the Stone Hill River. You'll have to get your feet wetter, I'm afraid, but it's only a small stream, not deep. We turn right, here."

"Golly, it's cold!" Dorothy splashed into the water behind him.

"Brrr—I know it. Lift your feet high or you'll fall over these boulders. And please try to make as little noise as possible."

From the direction of the woodlot came a prodigious crashing and threshing. The pursuit had gained the woods.

"Noise!" she said scornfully, floundering along in his wake. "Those thugs can't hear me—they're making too much racket themselves. I suppose, Bill, you're working on a plan, but what it can be is a mystery to me."

"You mean—where we're bound for?"

"Yes. We can't get back to the big pasture and the hill up to Stoker's house. They'll head off any play of that kind."

"I know that. Stand still a minute, I want to listen."

"But Bill—"

"Sh—yes, that must be it!"

"Must be what?" There was impatience in Dorothy's tone.

"The waterfall I was trying to find."

"You don't mean to tell me you're planning to crawl behind a waterfall and hide! Honestly, Bill, I—"

"Oh, nothing like that," he answered coolly, "the fall isn't big enough."

"Look here, will you *please*—"

"All right, calm yourself. We haven't much time but I guess they've lost our trail for the time being. On the way over here in the car, Terry told me something of the lay of the land. He's crazy about hiking, you know, and mountain climbing. He's walked all over the reservation and he knows it like his own back yard."

"Yes, yes, what of it?"

"Well, Terry told me that there is just one possible way to get out of this Stony Hill River Valley on this side. That is, unless one goes a mile or two up or down the valley. There are entrances to the reservation at either end—dirt roads that cross from the concrete turnpike over to this ridge above us."

"But there is a way out?"

"Yes. A sort of trail up the cliffs. It's not marked on the map of the reservation. Terry found it last summer. Pretty tough going even in daylight, I guess."

"But how on earth can we find it in the dark?"

"Terry told me that a smaller stream flowed into this creek at just about this point, and that it drops into the river gully by way of a low waterfall. It was the sound of that fall I was listening for. Hear it just over there to the right?"

"What's the next move?"

"We turn our backs on the waterfall, and cross this stream. The trail starts in a kind of open chimney in the foot of the cliffs. The map calls these young precipices Raven Rocks, by the way. If you think it is too dangerous, we can let those chaps catch us. They'll probably let us go soon enough. They're trailing the wrong party, though they haven't realized it. What do you say?" Bill's tone was non-committal.

"I know, they took you for Stoker Conway. But don't you see, Bill—" her tone was firm, "they must not find out their mistake. While they're tracking us, they will leave the Conway house alone, and that'll give Terry and Stoker a chance to hunt for the book and the letter."

Bill's reply was flippant, but there was a note of relief in his voice. "Chance to get a good night's rest, you mean!"

"They're not going to bed—" Dorothy pulled her companion toward the opposite bank of the stream. "Terry told me so."

"Thank goodness we're out of that," she exclaimed a moment later as they climbed the steep side of the gully. "If there's anything colder than a trout stream, I've yet to find it. I'm soaked nearly to my waist— how about you?"

"Ditto. We'll be warm enough presently—just as soon as we hit Raven Rocks."

"Wish we had raven's wings—we could use 'em!"

"Listen!" Bill stopped suddenly in his tracks.

"Don't *say* that," she whispered—"reminds me of old man Lewis!"

"They're coming this way. I guess they got tired of beating the woods for us. Take my hand again. We've got to find that chimney."

They went perhaps ten paces more when Bill brought up short again.

"Here's the cliff—wait where you are—be back in a minute."

He drew his fingers from her clasp and she heard him move off. Standing in utter darkness she could hear the men splashing toward them along the shallow river bed, and still others tramping through the woods with flashing lights that moved nearer every second.

Not once did her alert mind question the advisability of trying to scale Raven Rocks on a coal-black night. Not once did she waste a thought on the danger of that perilous enterprise. Dorothy Dixon never counted the cost when it was to help a friend. Her entire attention was centered on their pursuers. Who they were, or why they sought George and his letter were points of little consequence now. All that mattered was that they be kept on their search for as many hours as possible.

Presently they would come abreast and their lights would pick her out at the foot of the cliff. The sopping skirt of her frock sagged about her knees, dank and clammy beneath her slicker. She gathered it in her hands and squeezed what water she could from it, more for want of something to do than for any other reason.

No longer could she hear Bill stumbling about. What could have happened to him? The lights were only a dozen yards away now. In another minute or two their glare would pick her up for a certainty.

For the first time that evening, Dorothy became fidgety. Bill had told her to remain here. That was an order, and must be obeyed. But—oh! if Bill would only come!

Chapter VIII

THE CHIMNEY

Then on her right she heard a soft rustling, immediately followed by a low call:

"Dorothy, where are you?"

The words brought her joyous relief. "Coming!" she replied in a cautious whisper, and with her left hand feeling the almost sheer wall, she hurried toward Bill's voice.

From the darkness he grasped her hand and spoke close to her ear. "I've located the chimney, Dorothy."

"Good! I was getting worried. Is it far away?"

"No. Only a few steps."

"What kept you so long, Bill?"

"Had to find the rope."

"What rope?"

They were moving now in the direction from which he had come.

"The one Terry hid in a niche of the

rocks. Talk of hunting needles in a—"

"But do we need it?"

"Couldn't risk the climb without it. You've never done any mountain scaling —I have."

"Well, what's the dope?"

They had stopped and Bill took her arm. "Here—let me knot this end around your waist. First, ditch the slicker, though. You won't be able to climb in that. I'll take care of it for the present."

He took her coat and she felt him make the rope secure.

"I'm tied to the other end," he told her.

"But what'll you do about my slicker, Bill? If we ever get to the top of the ridge, I'll need it."

Bill was busy and didn't answer for a moment. Then—"Your coat and mine are rolled up and lashed to my back," he explained. "I'm going first. I know more about this kind of thing than you, and my reach is longer. May have to pull you up the hard places. Don't be afraid to put weight on the rope when I give the word. But if you slip—yell."

He did not say that a slip on her part would in all probability pull him with her to crash on the rocky ground below. Bill Bolton did not believe in being an alarmist, but she understood just the same.

"Thanks, I'll do my best, Bill."

"Start climbing." His voice came from above her head and she felt a jerk on the rope. "This chimney is a fissure in the cliff, and it slants slightly upward, thank goodness. Reach above and get handholds on the rock projections first. Then pull yourself up, until you find a foothold. When you put your weight on your feet, press your legs against the side walls. That will keep you from slipping. Take it easy and rest as much as you like. This kind of thing can only be done slowly."

"I'm coming," Dorothy said quietly and she pressed her body into the niche she could not see.

"That's the stuff!" I'll rest while you climb. And while you're doing it, I'll keep the rope taut and out of your way."

Dorothy was silent. Groping in the darkness above her head, her fingers came in contact with a rough projection. It was little more than a small knob in the rocky side of the chimney, but she managed to get a firm grip on it with her right hand. Her left found another projection slightly lower on the other side. She exerted all her strength and slithered upward.

Drawing her knees up she sought rests for her feet on the sides, but the rock seemed absolutely smooth. For an instant she was at a loss. Then remembering Bill's advice, she pressed her legs against the chimney walls and pushed.

That her body moved upward so easily came as a surprise. It was hard to realize that sheer walls would give such a purchase. Almost at once her shoulders were above the hand holds and she could raise herself by pressing downward until her left knee was planted on the same projection that she had gripped with that hand.

Braced firmly against the rock, she looked for higher hand holds, found them and soon was able to get her left foot on to the place where her knee had been. With her weight on that foot, it became a simple matter to plant her right in the opposite niche. Straightening her body, she lay forward against the slanting cliff and rested.

"Go ahead, Bill," she called in a low voice as soon as she could speak.

"O. K., kid," came the prompt reply from overhead. "On my way."

Pressed against the wet rockface she could hear the scrape of his boots and the heavy breathing of muscular strain. Her own thin soled shoes were sodden from the wet of the woods and pasture. Worse still, the leather was bursting at the sides. And this climb would probably complete their ruin. By the time she reached the top, they would be beyond walking in at all. Never again would she board her plane shod in pumps.

"Come along!"

Bill interrupted her soliloquy, and using the same tactics as before she continued to climb.

The first drops of rain she had felt at the bottom of the cliff now increased to a steady downpour. Dorothy became soaked to the skin. Water from her leather helmet ran down her forehead, forcing her to keep her eyes closed most of the time.

The cliff, wet and slippery from the preceding storm, was soon slick as a greased slide. Twice she lost her foothold and would have fallen had not her sharp cry warned Bill in time. How he managed to stick to his precarious perch and bear her weight on the rope until she found a grip on the rock again was more than she could fathom. Each time she slipped her heart almost stopped beating. And the horrible emptiness at the pit of her stomach made her feel deathly ill. But she never wholly lost her nerve. Climbing, then resting, she kept steadily on.

But her strenuous exertions and the almost continuous strain on muscles ordinarily little used was wearing down her vitality. Would this terrible climbing in the dark never end, she thought. Her whole body ached, her arms and legs felt heavy as lead. Wearily she raised her right hand seeking another hold. When she felt Bill's fingers grasp her own, she started. The shock very nearly caused her to lose balance.

"Now your other paw," said his well-known voice somewhere above in the gloom. "That's the way—up you come."

Then before she really understood what was happening, Dorothy was dragged higher until she was seated beside Bill on a narrow ledge. His right arm held her tightly. He was puffing like a grampus.

She wriggled and wiped the water and perspiration from her eyes with a wet, clammy hand.

"Sit tight—old girl," Bill's words came in little jerks. "I know you're used to altitudes in a plane, but this is different. I guess you'll get a shock when you look below, so—steady."

Dorothy opened her eyes and was glad of his supporting arm. Far below, at the foot of the cliff, pinpoints of light moved hither and yon, puncturing the darkness.

"They know we're somewhere up here," he said softly. "Heard you when you slipped, I dare say. Well, we'll take some finding—and that's no lie," he chuckled.

"Why—I—I—had no idea we'd come so far," she stammered. "Those lights look miles away."

"Three or four hundred feet, that's all."

"Funny—it makes me almost dizzy to look down there. You're right—it is different from flying altitude. Bill, do you think they'll find the chimney?"

"Maybe. But they're not likely to try to use it—not tonight, anyway."

"Why not? We did it."

"We were sure of a way up—they aren't. And I don't imagine they bargained for any blind climb up cliffs like these in the rain and darkness. They wouldn't mind slugging one of us with a sand bag, but when it comes to real danger, they'd count themselves out."

"Gee," Dorothy giggled nervously. "I wish I'd been able to!"

"Count yourself out? Well, I don't blame you, kid. Nerve-wracking isn't the name for it. But you certainly stood up well. Do you feel able to go on now?"

"Yes, I suppose so." Her reply was rather weak.

"Then we'd better get under way. Terry said the chimney was the worst of it and we are through with that now. It ends at this ledge." He helped her to her feet. "Brrr—that wind is cold on wet clothes. If we don't get moving, we'll cop a dose of pneumonia, sure as shooting!"

"You're a nice, thoughtful fella, Bill," Dorothy smiled grimly in his direction. "Trouble is your thoughtfulness is oddly strenuous at times. Is there much farther to go?"

"We're more than half way," he assured her, "and from now on you'll get more walking than climbing."

Dorothy wanted to laugh but was too tired to do so.

"Lead on, MacDuffer," she cried gamely. "I'm lame, halt and blind, but I'll do my best to follow my chief!"

"Atta girl," he commended. "Give us your paw again, we can travel better that way."

"We'll travel, all right—that is, unless our friend Terry is a dyed-in-the-wool fabricator."

"Hopefully not, as they say in the Fatherland," he chuckled. He caught her hand in his and they started on a climb up the steep hill that ran back from the ledge.

As Bill had predicted, the going here was not nearly so difficult as it had been in the chimney. So far as Dorothy could tell, the cliffs, which were covered with a grass-grown rubble, sloped in at this point, and at a much easier angle of ascent. Whereas the chimney was almost perpendicular, here, by bending forward and aiding progress with occasional handholds on bushes and rocky outcroppings, it was possible to do more than merely creep forward.

A slip, of course, would be dangerous. It would be hard to stop rolling, once started down the incline; and unless a bush or a boulder were conveniently in the way, a bound over the ledge would be inevitable —and then oblivion.

She did not like to think about it. Bill guided her up the incline and did so with uncanny accuracy, considering the darkness, and the fact that he had not travelled this trail before. She came to the conclusion that the worst was over, when he stopped abruptly.

"Sit down and take it easy," he advised. "This is where I've got to see what we're doing."

"Surely you're not going to show a light?" she asked in alarm, and sank down on the rocky ground.

"Have to," was his quick reply. "Those guys below us know we're up here, so what does it matter?"

"But I thought we were almost at the top."

"Almost, but not quite. Look at that!"

A beam of light shot upward from his torch, and turning her head, she saw a sight that sent her heart down to the very tips of her ragged, soaking pumps.

They had indeed come to the top; but merely to the top of this steep hillside of bushes and rubble. Where this ended, a few feet away, the naked rock towered almost perpendicular. Forty feet or more from its base this wall jutted sharply outward, half that distance again.

She sprang to her feet, an exclamation of dismay on her lips.

This rock canopy above their heads, this absolutely unscalable barrier to their hopes extended in both directions so far as the eye could see.

Bill, who had moved several feet downhill, was flashing his light back and forth along the rugged edge of this roof of rock beneath which she stood.

"How far does it go?" she asked in a small voice.

"According to Terry," he replied, "right to where the cliffs end—both ways—and without a break or a tunnel. But you can't walk along underneath very far, because this slant we are on is only forty or fifty yards wide. Beyond it in either direction there's a sheer drop."

"Then—we're out of luck." Her tone was entirely hopeless.

Bill laughed shortly. "Where Terry got down, we can get up—but it's not going to be easy—and that's sure fire!"

Chapter IX

OVER THE TOP

"Well! If you know the way out, why don't you say so?" Dorothy flared in exasperation.

"What?" returned Bill vaguely.

He was walking across the side of the hill, keeping beneath the end of the rocky overhang forty feet above his head. The light from his electric torch swept along the edge of this seemingly unsurmountable obstruction. Then it darted out and upward as if to pierce the dripping night above.

"Did you speak?" he amended, looking back at her. "Thought I heard you say something, but couldn't quite catch it."

His voice was as sincere as the words he had just uttered, but Dorothy's reply was caustic.

"I said why keep the secret to yourself? All this stuff about how Terry got down and we are supposed to get up is keeping me on pins and needles. If Terry left a rope ladder or something hanging over the edge last summer, it must be gone by now."

"No, he didn't use a rope ladder—"

"Well, it looks to me as if we'd have to fly up if we ever want to get to the top of this ridge! I don't know whether you're *trying* to tantalize me—but you're succeeding, all right. For goodness' sake, Bill, if you know the answer, tell me."

"I'm sorry, Dorothy," he called repentantly. He ran up the incline toward her. "I didn't mean to leave you in the soup— I ought to have realized—Look, I'm awfully sorry," he repeated in sincere contrition.

"Oh, that's all right, Bill." She was embarrassed now. "I had no business to get so shirty." Under the light of the torch, their eyes met in a smile of friendly understanding.

"But please tell me what it is you're trying to find?"

"Why, the tree—I honestly thought I'd told you about it before."

"What tree?" she asked patiently.

"The one that Terry used to get down here. It's our only hope."

"But I don't see any tree. If there is one, how is it going to help us?"

Bill took her hand and gave it a little pat.

"Come over here with me," he said, and led the way toward the spot where he had been standing.

"But Bill—there's no tree up there—"

"Wait until I get the light on it. There you are!"

And there was a tree, after all. But instead of pointing toward the heavens like any other tree she had ever seen, this Colorado spruce grew sideways out from the top of the cliff. With the exception of a few tufts on the top, its branches grew only on the upper side of the horizontal trunk, giving it more the appearance of a ragged hedge than an honest-to-goodness tree.

"I get you," she said slowly. "The tree —and the rope."

"Aha! young lady, you're not so dumb as you'd sometimes like people to think!"

"But is the rope long enough?"

"Hope so. Terry claimed he used it double."

"Yes?" she said doubtfully. "But will the tree hold us both? You've been a sailor, but I don't think I'm up to climbing a swinging rope, hand over hand after coming up that chimney." She thought for a moment, then went on. "There's only one way I can get up there. You'll have to tie one end of the rope to a stone and sling it over the trunk. When that end drops, we can take out the stone, I'll stick my foot in the loop and—"

"Bill Bolton pulls you up," he ended for her. "That listens well, Dorothy, and if the rope was running through a pulley up there, everything would be hunky-dory. As it is, she'll be chafing against a hard, uneven surface. I'd probably pull the tree down, even if I was able to get you off the ground."

"But my arms feel dead—right up to my shoulders."

"I know, kid. But you can do it, after I fix the rope and you have lashed your end to this big bush here. It's going to be a case of shin for you, not hand over hand climb. Although that's not so hard when you know how. Like most things, there's a knack to it."

"All right. I'll do my best."

"You'll make it," he assured her. "If you'll untie that end of the rope from around your waist, I'll hunt up a rock and we'll get busy."

Presently a heavy stone was fastened to the rope end.

"Stand clear," sang out Bill. Then as she stepped back, he swung the stone round and round in a vertical circle, much as a seaman heaves the lead for a sounding.

Up went the stone and the rope, and Dorothy watched with bated breath while she pointed the torch for guidance. She saw it swing over the tree trunk and drop to earth on the farther side.

"Snappy work, Bill," she applauded. "Who goes first? You or me?"

"This is a case where gentlemen take precedence. I'll go first—and show you a little trick they teach midshipmen at Annapolis."

He untied the knot which held the stone and bringing the ends together pulled the rope until the lengths on both sides of the trunk were even.

"So long," he breezed, "see you anon!"

With a hand on either rope he swung himself upward, seemingly without effort. It was as though he were lifting a penny-weight rather than one hundred and seventy-five pounds of solid American bone and muscle. Then with a quick movement he twisted the slack ends about his thighs, and the girl was amazed to see him let go both hands and wave.

"It's a way we have in the Navy," he laughed. "Quite a comfortable seat—if you know how. Skirts are rather in the way, so I don't advise you to try it. Although I must say in parting that you have already parted with the greater part of your skirt."

Dorothy giggled. "What of it? There's a perfectly good pair of bloomers underneath." She was amused by his fooling, though she suspected he was trying to put heart into her.

Bill coughed. "Finicky persons of British extraction might claim that your last statement was a decided bloomer itself—but I digress—" he went on, in the manner of a barker at a side show. "Laydees and gen-tel-men—I wish to state that William Bolton, late tiddledywinks champion of the Nutmeg State, is about to give his famous impersonation of a monkey on a stick!"

His hands grasped the ropes above his head. Up came his body, the turns about his thighs providing an apparently comfortable seat or purchase, while his hands shot upward again. The speed with which he went through these movements was remarkable, the swiftness of his passage up the ropes only comparable to an East Indian running up a cocoanut palm. Before Dorothy could believe her eyes, he was sitting astride the tree trunk, hauling up the rope.

"That was marvelous!" she called up to him. "Some day you'll have to show me how you do it."

"O. K.!"

She saw now that one end of the rope

was coming slowly down again. As it sank nearer, her torch brought to view the fact that it was knotted every few feet. Soon she was able to catch the swinging end.

"Make it fast to that bush," he commanded.

She did as she was told and turned to him for further orders.

Bill pulled the rope taut, then lashed his end about the trunk close to the point where the tree jutted out from the rock. That done he slashed the loose half free with his knife just above the knot.

"That gives us a hauling line," she heard him say. "I'll hang on to this end—you knot the other about your waist."

She caught the end that he threw down and after fastening it securely about her, peered up at him again.

"All right for me to shin up?" she asked, with a hand on the knotted rope that was to act as her ladder to the dizzy height above.

"Wait till I get back on terra firma—this tree won't stand our combined weights."

Perhaps a minute elapsed.   Then she

heard his voice again, though she could no longer see him.

"Come ahead!" he directed. "Sing out when you start and let me know if I pull too hard."

Dorothy switched off the light and slipped the torch down the back of her frock where it was caught in the blouse made by the line about her waist.

"Ready!" she called and grasping the taut rope, she started to shin up.

Almost immediately she was helped on her way by a steady pull on the line Bill was holding. The going was difficult but the knots held her and kept her from slipping. Notwithstanding aching arm and leg muscles, it was surprising how easily she was able to hoist herself upward with the added pull from above. The actual distance to be climbed was not so great, but it seemed unbelievably soon when her hands touched the tree trunk.

Bill called a warning. "Get a good purchase around the rope with your legs, then lift your arms—take hold of the branches on top of the trunk and heave!"

She felt a stronger pull on the rope; her hands grasped two upright branches and she was dragged upward and on to the tree. Bill caught her under her arms and swung her on to the rock. Then he picked her up bodily and carried her back a few yards from the edge of the chasm.

"Hurray! We're up!" he gasped and let her down on solid ground.

Dorothy did not reply. For a moment speech was beyond her. She sank down on a boulder. After a little while she untied the rope that belted her and producing the electric torch, handed it to Bill.

"Snap on the light, will you?—while I take stock of the damage. I know I'm a wreck, but it's just as well to learn the worst at once."

"Rather rumpled," he pronounced as he complied with her request. "Good night! You've only got one shoe!"

"Lost the other coming up the rope. This one is no good either. What's left of it is just a mass of soaking pulp."

Then she laughed softly as she brushed some spruce needles from her knees and picked a malicious little bit of flint from the palm of one hand. Her wet skirt was in ribbons. She saw that her stockings were a mass of ladders now, and she had a suspicion that her knickers were torn. But what did such trifles matter when one was bent upon a great achievement?

"Pretty bad," she admitted and stood up on one foot. "Hand me my slicker, please. This rig is beyond repair—that will keep some of the wind out. Gee, it's chilly!"

"And wet," he added grimly, as he helped her into the coat. "Sorry to have to remind you, Dorothy, but we've got to be on our way, again."

"I don't think I can go any further, Bill."

He knew this to be a candid statement of fact, not a complaint.

"But we must, Dorothy. They are coming after us, you know."

"Not up this cliff! Unless, you mean—" her voice was troubled, "the rope! Could you slide down ours and untie that from the bushes, then shin up again?"

"I could, but it isn't necessary. They aren't coming that way."

"Is there another way?"

"Yes, for them. By the road across the valley and around by either of the entrances to the reservation."

"Why are you so sure?"

"Because while I was out on the tree trunk, I saw lights going up the hill. Then a car which evidently had been parked down the road from Stoker's house, started off toward the Boutonville entrance. Which means, of course, that they'll motor in on the Boutonville road. That crosses the reservation. Then all they've got to do is to leave the car at the mouth of the Fire Tower trail and hike down here along the top of the cliffs. They've cut off any retreat down the cliffs on our part, too. Those birds intend to catch us—or rather, they want to get hold of Stoker pretty badly. They've left men down in the valley, I saw their lights."

"Well, it will take them some time to walk over here from the Boutonville road," Dorothy said wearily. "I'm going to sleep. I've got to."

"You can't—not in this rain. And

you're soaked through into the bargain."
Bill's tone was firm. "Wait a minute—I've
got an idea."

Dorothy, who was half dozing with her
back to the boulder, opened her eyes with
an effort. She saw him draw forth a paper
from his pocket, unfold it and study it with
the aid of the lighted torch.

"This is a map of Poundridge Reservation," he explained. "Here's a trail that
leads back from Raven Rocks to the Spy
Rock Trail. This end of it must be about
a hundred yards along the cliffs to our left,
if I've got my bearings right. Listen,
Dorothy! These two trails meet about a
mile and a half from here—and close by is
a cabin. It's marked Shelter No. 6 on the
map. Once in there we'll be under cover.
These shelters are rented to campers during the summer, you know. There's sure
to be a fireplace. I'll find the dry wood and
we can dry out and get warm."

Dorothy yawned and shut her eyes
again.

"No use, Bill. I hate to be a short
sport—but I'm just all in. Chances are

we'd find the cabin locked when we got there."

Bill put the map back in his pocket.

"I don't blame you," was what he said. "I'm used to roughing it and I don't feel any too scrumptious myself. But we've got to do something. The gang will be here in less than an hour. But I must admit that I don't see how you're going to walk a mile and a half with only one shoe."

He looked down at Dorothy. She was fast asleep.

Chapter X

OL' MAN RIVER

"Poor kid! She certainly is all in," Bill muttered in a tone that was close to despair. What on earth was he going to do now?

The wind had stiffened and heavy rain slanted out of the east in an unremitting deluge. Both of them were soaked to the skin under their slickers. Despite his vigorous cliff-climbing, Bill was chilled to the very marrow of his bones, and he saw that Dorothy, huddled against the boulder, was shivering in her sleep.

He himself was weary and heavy-eyed. His vitality was at low ebb. But with a sudden exertion of latent will power he got painfully to his feet. He bent over the sleeping girl and taking her by the shoulders shook her back and forth.

"Wake up, Dorothy!" he called. "Wake up!"

Deep in oblivion, she made no answer. Bill shook her harder.

"Leave me 'lone," she murmured drowsily. "Want sleep—go 'way!"

Putting forth his full strength, Bill lifted her until she stood leaning against him still sound asleep. Bringing her arms up and over his shoulders, he pivoted in a half circle. Now that his back was toward her, he bent forward, and catching her legs, drew them over his thighs. Dorothy, still oblivious to all that went on, was hoisted up into the position called by small children, "riding piggy-back." Though slender, she was well-built and muscular, and he was surprised at her dead weight. With his forearms beneath her knees, clutching the lighted torch with one hand, he moved slowly off with her in the direction of the Raven Rock Trail.

After some little trouble he found it, a narrow swath cutting back through the forest at right angles to the top of the cliffs. Without hesitation he began to follow the path.

Overhead the twisted branches met in

a natural arch. It seemed even darker below their dripping foliage than in the open on the cliffs, and the feeble ray from his flash light penetrated but a few feet into the yawning black ahead. It was heavy going with Dorothy's solid weight on his back. The uneven ground, sodden with rain, was slippery where his feet did not sink in the muddy loam. And at times he was near to falling with his burden.

The trail followed a snakelike course. For a time it wound over comparatively level ground, then dipped steeply into a hollow. The girl was becoming heavier by the minute. Bill stuck it out until they topped the opposite rise, then let her down.

Dorothy awoke with a start.

"What are you doing?" she cried. "Where am I?"

"So far as I can make out, we're about half a mile down the Raven Rock trail," he said slowly.

"And—and you carried me all this way?"

"Piggyback," he replied laconically.

"Why, Bill! You must be nearly dead—"

"Well, there have been times when I've felt more peppy—"

"How could you, Bill? Why didn't you wake me up?"

"Tried to—but it just wasn't any use. You couldn't have walked it, anyway—with only one shoe."

"Oh, yes, I could. But you were sweet to do it, only—"

"Better climb aboard again," he suggested, ignoring her praise, "we've got all of a mile to go before we get to the cabin."

Dorothy made a gesture of dissent.

"Thanks, old dear. I'm going to walk."

"Well, if you feel up to it—you take my shoes—I'll get along fine without them in this mud."

"I'll do nothing of the kind. I've got a better plan. Stupid of me not to think of it before. Hand over your knife, please."

Dorothy cut two long strips, six or seven inches wide, from the bottom of her slicker. "I'm going to use these to bind up my feet," she explained and handed back the knife.

"Wait a minute!"

Bill seized his own raincoat and cut two

wider strips, which he folded into pads.

"Sit down on that stump, and hold up your hoof," he ordered. "I'll show you how it's done."

Dorothy hopped to the stump and after seating herself, kicked off her remaining shoe.

"There goes the end of a perfect pump," she chuckled.

"Think I'll keep it for luck," declared Bill.

She raised her eyebrows and laughed.

"Some girls might think you were becoming sentimental—you, of all people!"

"Well?"

"Well, I know it's only because you were born practical. You want that shoe so as to prevent anyone else from finding it, the men who are chasing us, for instance?"

"I never argue with members of the opposite sex—that's why I still enjoy good health."

He grinned and pocketed the shoe.

"Hold up your foot, young lady. It's a lovely night and all that, but we're going to get out of it as soon as possible."

He placed one of the folded pads beneath the sole of her foot and wound a strip of slicker about it and the foot bringing the ends together in a knot about her ankle.

"Now the other," he prompted, and dealt with it in the same way.

Dorothy stood up and took a trial step or two.

"Wonderful!" she said. "I could walk to New York in these. They're a lot more comfortable than the shoes I ordinarily wear."

"We'll have to patent the idea."

"That reminds me, Bill," Dorothy spoke slowly. They were moving along the trail again. "Do you think the letter Mr. Conway is supposed to have written Stoker could possibly have had anything to do with patents?"

"What patents?"

"Oh, I don't know exactly—patents belonging to Mr. Conway."

"You mean—which he left to Stoker?"

"Why, yes. Mr. Conway was an inventor. He must have patented things."

"Very probably. But Stoker told us that

his father's entire estate amounted to the place he's living in and a few thousand dollars. If Mr. Conway still owned patent rights on his inventions, why weren't they mentioned in the will?"

"You think, then, that he sold them before his death?"

"Looks that way," summed up Bill. "Anyway, if there were patents, they'd be registered in Washington. It wouldn't do anyone any good to steal them."

Dorothy tramped along beside him. Except for the sound of their footsteps squishing in the muddy path and the drip of the rain from wet leaves and branches, the woods were very still.

"What can those people be after if it isn't the patents on Mr. Conway's inventions?" she said in a puzzled tone, after a pause.

"Search me—what ever it is, the thing must be very valuable. They'd never take all this trouble otherwise."

"Give us all this trouble, you mean. And here's another riddle, Bill. Why was Hilltop sold?"

Bill threw her a glance and shrugged.

"Ask me something real hard," he suggested. "You're the Sherlock Holmes of this case. I'm only a mighty dumb Doctor Watson. And I'm no good at problems in deduction, even when my thinkbox is moting properly—which it isn't at present."

"But there must have been some good reason for the sale of that property," she persisted. "When Stoker went back to Lawrenceville after the Easter holidays last spring, everything at home was going on just as usual—a big place, servants, cars, horses, plenty of money—everything. Then he came back from school in June, and all that everything just wasn't!"

"And father had moved into that dump on the Stone Hill River road with a part-time maid-of-all-work, and that 1492 flivver. . . . Deucedly clear and all that! By the way, do they teach English or just plain Connecticut Yankee at the New Canaan High? Your use of words at times is more forceful than grammatic."

"Grammatical for choice. You're not

so hot on the oratory yourself, Bill. People who live in glass houses, you know—?"

"Wish we were in one," was his reply. "Anything with a fire and a roof that sheds water would suit me just now!"

"What are you trying to do, Bill, evade my question?"

Dorothy's nap had done her good. Though still weary and stiff, she felt tantalizingly argumentative for all that she was wringing wet and horribly chilly. Talking helped to keep up her spirits. Just ahead their torch revealed a branching of the path.

"The map says we keep to the right," announced Bill. "It's only a step over to the Spy Rock trail now."

"Glad to hear it—but it seems to me you *are* trying to evade my questions!"

"Questions?" He chuckled. "They come too fast and furious. And to be honest, how can you expect me to guess the right answers when you don't know them yourself? You certainly are the one and only human interrogation point tonight."

"And you're so helpful," she retorted.

"This is the most mysterious affair I've ever been mixed up in."

"Here we are at the other trail, praise be to Allah."

"Turn to the right?" she asked.

"That's it. In about a hundred yards we ought to run on to a path leading off to the left. That leads to shelter No. 6. The cabin's quite near now, if this map in my pocket's any good."

They trudged along the trail and a couple of minutes later in the dim glow from the flash they saw an opening in the trees.

"Come on," he said, quickening his pace. "We'll be under cover in a jiffy."

"We'll probably have to break in." Dorothy caught up with him as the path swung round in a quarter circle to the left.

"No, we won't," he replied, catching her arm and coming to a halt. At the same time he shut off the electric torch.

Straight ahead in the darkness they could make out the blur of a small building. Through a chink in what they took to be a closed shutter came a thin ray of light.

"Somebody's got there ahead of us," Bill observed more to himself than to Dorothy.

"What are we going to do?"

"Do? What can we do but knock them up and ask for shelter?"

"I guess you're right," she admitted. "Neither of us can go on until we've had rest and a drying out."

"That's how I look at it."

"We've got to go easy, though. Remember what I trotted into with Betty at Stoker's house?"

"Where do you get this 'we' stuff?" he said rather gruffly. "Here, take this gun and get behind a tree. I'm going over there. If they get nasty when they open up, I'll sidestep—and you can use your own judgment."

"I'll use it right now, Bill. I'm going to the house with you. Don't argue—" She started on along the path.

Bill caught up with her. "Take the automatic, anyway," he shoved the gun into her hand. "Shoot through your pocket if you have to. Better keep it out of sight. Stand to one side just out of the line of light when they open. All set?"

"Go ahead."

Dorothy's right hand gripped the revolver in her pocket. She slipped off the safety catch, pointed her forefinger along the snubnosed barrel and let her middle finger rest lightly on the trigger.

Rat-tat-tat—rat-tat-tat.   Bill's fist pounded the cabin door. There came a pause. She felt the quickened beats of her heart. Rain pounding on the gutterless roof dripped in a steady trickle on her bare head and down her neck. From somewhere nearby came the mournful cry of a hoot owl.

Bill knocked again. Within the little house they heard the sound of footsteps. Dorothy stiffened.

The bolts of the door were withdrawn, the door opened and Dorothy stepped up beside Bill. Framed in the lighted rectangle was an ancient, white haired negro. He peered out at them from beneath the cotton-tufts of his eyebrows, blinded for the moment by the night.

"Good evening, Uncle. Can we come in out of the wet for a little while?"

Bill's tone held the gentle camaraderie of those brought up by darky servants in the South.

"Lordy, Lordy—white folks, an' drippin' wet!" exclaimed the old fellow, straightening his bent back and smiling pleasantly. "Walk right in, Capt'in—and you, too, Missy. Ol' Man River ain't got quarters like you is prob'ly useter—But it's dry and it's warm, an' yo-all's sho' is welcome!"

Chapter XI

MR. JOHN J. JOYCE

"Thank you, Uncle," said Bill and motioning Dorothy to go first, he stepped across the threshold.

The old darky slammed the door shut behind them blotting out the storm, and sent the bolt home.

"Yo'all go over ter the fire an' drip," he beamed, pointing to the blazing logs in the fireplace of native stone. "Lordy, Lordy, you chillen is sho' 'nuf half drown'. But we's gwine ter fix dat sho' nuf in a jiffy."

While the two warmed their hands at the hearth, he bustled off towards the rear of the cabin and disappeared through a doorway that led into another room.

Dorothy looked at Bill and smiled delightedly.

The cabin was primitive though there was a cozy and homelike air about it. The chinks between the bark of the logs which formed the walls were stuffed with dry moss and clay. There was no ceiling to the room. One looked up through the cross beams clear to the gable of the slanting roof. From these sturdy four-by-fours hung half a ham, several bunches of onions, a pair of rubber boots and other oddments. Wide boards had been laid across them in a couple of places, evidently to provide holdalls for other paraphernalia.

The small room's principal article of furniture was a rustic, handmade table. Three stools without backs and an armchair of like manufacture completed the furnishings if one did not count several shining pots and pans that hung on nails driven into the logs and a huge pile of kindling that took up an entire corner. A steaming kettle hung from a crane over the fire and the floor of the room flaunted a large mat woven of brightly colored grasses.

"He keeps everything as neat as a new pin," Dorothy whispered. "Isn't he perfectly sweet?"

"Wonder how he happens to be here,"

said Bill. "This shelter is state property."

"Shush—he's coming."

The old darky ambled into the room again, grinning from ear to ear. Ol' Man River, as he called himself, quite evidently enjoyed bestowing hospitality. Over one arm he carried a bundle of clothes.

"Ise mighty thankful dat yo'all come 'long dis evenin'," he exclaimed. "It sho' do get mighty lonesome up in dese hyar woods—speshally on a black night when de rain come an' de wind howl roun' dis cabin. I brought you all some clo's. 'Twant much I could find, jes' overalls and shirts, like what Ise got on. But dey is dry and dey is as clean an' sweet as soap and rainwater can make 'em."

Dorothy took the faded blue flannel shirt and overalls he held out to her. "Thank you, Uncle. You certainly are kind and thoughtful, but it's a shame to use your clean clothes this way."

The old man's grin grew wider, his even white teeth gleamed in the wrinkled black of his kindly face.

"Don' you menshun it, Missy. Dese

clo's ain't nuffin. Dey ain't no tellin'
what's gwine ter happen ef you don' hop
inter de back room an' take off yo' wet
things. While yo' gone, de young genneman can change. An' Ol' Man River, he's
gwine ter dish up supper. Now, Missy,
run away or yo'll sho' catch yo' death in
dose wet things."

Dorothy hurried into the back room and
closed the door. On a little table she saw
an old fashioned oil lamp with a glass base
and an unshaded chimney, which cast a
cheerful glow of light over a home-made
bed which filled one side of the cubicle.
As she sat down, she found that instead of
a mattress, the bed boasted fir and hemlock
boughs, scented and springy to the touch.
Several khaki-colored army blankets were
neatly rolled at the foot of the bed. A row
of hooks behind the door and rudely fashioned shelves which extended the breadth
of the partition between the two rooms,
completed the appointments of Ol' Man
River's bedroom.

Dorothy saw that the partition did not
rise clear to the peak of the roof, but ended

at the crossbeams. The sound of Bill's voice and the old darky's came over the top, and a most appetizing odor of coffee and frying ham. It was just then that Dorothy realized how famished she was. A glance at her wristwatch showed that it was a quarter past midnight.

She continued to strip off her wet clothes and the wrappings from her feet. Picking up a couple of flour sacks from the stool by the shuttered window, she gave herself a thorough rub down. The home-made towels had been washed until they were soft as linen, and they sent a pleasant glow of returning circulation throughout her tired body. Warm and dry once more, she donned the overalls and shirt and drew on a heavy pair of gray wool socks. Though the overalls needed turning up and the shirt was too long in the sleeves and more than a trifle wide across her shoulders, it was on the whole a warm and comfortable outfit.

She rubbed her short, curly hair dry, then combed it into place before the cracked mirror which stood on the wall shelf. A deft application of powder and rouge from her ever-present compact completed her simple toilet. There came a knock on the door and Bill's voice told her that supper was ready.

"Coming!" she called.

Picking up the sodden heap of clothes from the floor, she blew out the light, opened the door and marched into the other room.

"Transformation!" Bill saluted her gaily. "How about it, Uncle Abe? You'd never take her for the same person, would you?"

The old man, who was bending over the hearth, turned his head toward her and smiled.

"Roses," he said, "roses in June!"

Dorothy laughed outright. "Thanks for the compliment, Uncle Abe, but I'm afraid these roses came out of a compact."

She hung her wet clothes over a chair, near to Bill's.

"Den I should'a said, fresh as a rose," the old darky chuckled.

"And not half as dewey as when you let

us in," added Bill. "By the way, Dorothy, let me introduce our host, Uncle Abe Lincoln River—known to the world at large as Ol' Man River, but to his friends he's Uncle Abe. And the young lady who is parading around in your clothes, Uncle, is Miss Dorothy Dixon of New Canaan, known to many people as I-will-not-be-called-Dot! She looks kind and gentle, but if you value your life, never take her on in a wrestling bout. She's Sandow, the Terrible Greek and the Emperor of Japan all in one."

Dorothy waved him aside.

"Get out of my way, slanderer!" she cried. "I want to shake hands with Uncle Abe. Dry clothes seem to have gone to his head, Uncle."

The aged negro stood up and took her outstretched hand between his horny palms.

"Why, I'se read about yo'all when I worked fo' Misteh Joyce, Missy. Dey uster let me hab de papers after de folks up dar ter de big house done finished wid 'em. Airplanes, robbers, ebbryt'ing!" Ol'

Man River shook his head. "Sho' wuz tuk back some ter see what ladies kin do dese days, ma'am!"

"Well, then you must have read about Mr. Bolton, here, too? Bill Bolton, the flyer—?"

"Dat's so, ma'am. I done heard tell o' dis genneman, too!" He turned his rolling eyes in unfeigned admiration upon Bill.

Bill glared at Dorothy. "Oho! so you put the spotlight on me, do you?" He cried in pretended anger.

But Ol' Man River motioned toward the table which was set with tin cups and plates and a very much battered metal coffee pot.

"Supper's ready, Missy. I'se sorry I ain't got a cloth. 'P'raps yo'all won't mind dis time. Now if yo' an' Marse' Bill will tak' yo' chairs, I'll serve it up quicker dan whistlin'."

"But you've only set two places," protested Dorothy.

Uncle Abe wagged his woolly pate. "It ain't right fo' an' ol' niggeh ter sit down wid de quality, Missy."

"Stuff and nonsense! Put another cup and plate on the table, Bill, and another knife, fork and spoon. Uncle Abe's going to eat with us, or I won't touch a thing— and believe me, this food looks tempting!"

"Well, if yo' puts it thataway, ma'am, I will take a bite." Uncle Abe gave a mellow chuckle. "I sho' duz love ham. De smell of it in de pan fair do make my mouf water!"

Dorothy took up the hot skillet from the hearth. "I'll put the ham on the plates, Uncle Abe, if you'll bring over that pan of hot bread you've got warming in the ashes."

"Not hot bread, Dorothy," corrected Bill, "—corn pone—real honest-to-goodness corn pone!"

"Mmmm—" she exclaimed with eyes dancing, "hurry up, Uncle Abe, I just can't wait!"

"Dey ain't no butter," explained Uncle Abe, "but if yo'all puts some o' dis ham gravy over it, I reckon yo'll fin' yo' kin eat it."

"Ho, that's the best way to eat it!" cried

Bill. "Used to have it that way when I lived at Annapolis. If there's anything that tastes better, I've yet to find it. And look, Dorothy, we've got molasses to sweeten our coffee! Uncle Abe sure does set a real southern table."

The old man chuckled happily as they sat down to the meal.

"Marse Johnson done give me dat 'lasses," he said as he filled the coffee cups from the battered pot. "He de big boss o' de reservation. I don't mind tellin' yo'-all, ma'am, if Marse Johnson didn't wink at Ol' Man River a-livin' in dis hyar cabin, dis niggeh sho' would be in a bad way. But dese reservation folks is no white trash. Dey knowed 'bout Marse Joyce turnin' me loose after I'd worked fo' him all dese years. I did odd jobs for 'em dis summer, an' a while back, Marse Johnson, he 'lowed I could have de cabin, now it's gettin' kinda chilly fo' de ol' man to sleep in de barn."

"That was pretty decent of him," remarked Bill, with his mouth full of fried ham and hot corn pone. "But who is this Mr. Joyce you speak of, Uncle?"

Ol' Man River wiped his mouth with the back of his hand.

"Dat man's name ez John J. Joyce, Marse Billy. He's got dat big place on de ridge over yonder nexter Hilltop, Marse Conway's ol' home. I worked fo' Marse Joyce fo' 'bout ten years—eveh sence I come up no'th from Virginny where dis ol' niggeh was raised."

"And he let you go after you'd worked for him all that time?" cried Dorothy, setting down her coffee cup. "I call that rotten mean!"

"Yaas, ma'am—John J. Joyce is sho' a hard man. I wuz one o' de gard'ners on de' 'state. One noon he calls us all up ter de big house. 'Men,' he say, standin' on de gall'ry steps, 'times is hard an' they's gwine ter be harder. I'se got ter do my bit fer dis 'ere depresshun like eve'y one else. Dat is why I'se a-cuttin' you down from six ter three. De three what am de oldest can clear out. Dey ain't wu'th as much ter me.'"

"The dirty dog!" Bill's face was hot with anger.

"I should say so!" Dorothy's tone matched Bill's in vehemence.

Uncle Abe shook his head. "De Good Book say, 'Him what has, gits, and him what ain't got nuffin' gits dat nuffin' tuk'n away'," he remarked a bit sadly. "But dis hyar niggeh ain't got no complaint, ma'am. Ol' Man River has sho' got a warm cabin. He ken trap Brer Rabbit in de woods, and 'times he gits Brer Possum. Marse Johnson pays fer a spell o' work once in a while and dat pays foh things he haster buy over to de store. I kinder git de idee, Missy, dat dis hyar ol' man is livin' on de top o' de worl'."

"Well, maybe," answered Dorothy, "but I call it doggone mean, just the same. Tell me, Uncle, outside of being mean and heartless, what sort of man is this John J. Joyce?"

"Waal, you see'd how he done me, Missy. Jes' git up an' go—didn't say he wuz sorry or nuffin'. He's rich and he's sharp. Maybe he's honest, I don't know, but I'se allus thought as how Marse Conway 'ud done better if he'd er hoed his

own 'taters.   But I reckon dis niggeh
hadn't oughter be crit'sizin' de quality."

"Quality, nothing!" exploded Bill. "Mr.
Conway was all right—at least, George
is—but the other fellow is the worst kind
of a polecat!"

"Den yo'all knows Marse George?"

"Yes, Uncle, he's a friend of ours," said
Dorothy.   "And he is right up to his neck
in trouble just now.   Anything you can
tell us about his father will be a big help."

Uncle Abe pushed his plate away and
leaned his elbows on the table.

"Dey ain't much I kin tell," he announced, "but I'se knowed Marse George
since he wuz a l'il boy. He wuz allus nice
an' friendly with Uncle Abe."

"You say that his father and Mr. Joyce
were friends—that they had dealings of
some sort together?" Dorothy inquired.

"Yaas, ma'am. Dey wuz pardners in
bizness, I reckon. Leastways, like you
said, dey had dealings togedder."

"But if Joyce was in business with Mr.
Conway, why didn't Stoker mention that?"
asked Bill of Dorothy.

"Perhaps he didn't know about it, Bill. He was away at school, remember, most of the time. And he told us that his father never spoke of his affairs or encouraged him to ask questions."

"But it doesn't sound reasonable, Dorothy. A fellow must know the name of his father's firm."

"That's true, in a way. But maybe there was no firm—of Joyce and Conway? Isn't it possible that Mr. Joyce may have acted as Mr. Conway's agent—sold the inventions for him, perhaps? Mr. Conway was not a business man. He was always too occupied in his laboratory or in his workshop."

"Dat am de way it wuz, Missy," broke in the old darky eagerly. "'Times, de gennemen 'ud walk in de garden an' talk while dis hyar niggeh done his weedin' or plantin' or wotnot—neveh done pay 'tenshun ter Ol' Man River. He don't count fer nuffin' atall. Marse Conway done make his 'ventions—Marse Joyce done what he call 'put 'em on de market.' Is dat what yo'all wanter know, ma'am?"

"Yes, thank you, Uncle.   I believe I'm beginning to see light at last."

"Blest if I do," commented Bill. "Joyce couldn't try to steal patents registered in Mr. Conway's name, could he?"

Dorothy smiled.   "That can wait.   It's time we helped Uncle Abe wash up. Then maybe he'll let us have a couple of blankets to spread before the fire.   We're dead for sleep and we're keeping him up too."

The old fellow started to answer, then cocked his head and lifted a warning hand.

"Is folks a-follerin' yo' chill'un?" he asked suddenly.

"Yes," said Dorothy, "and they mustn't catch us!"

"Dey's someone a-comin'," he whispered. "Don' yo' say nuffin'. Jes do like Uncle Abe tell yo'all and he fix it so nobody can't find nuffin' hyar!"

Chapter XII

VOICES FROM BELOW

"Take dose clo'es by de fire yonder," directed the sharp-eared old man, "an' go in de back room an' shin up de wall shelves to dese fo'-by fo's oveh our heads. Tote de clo'es 'long wid yo' an' lay flat on dem boards. 'Times I trap somefin' out er season—dis niggeh's got ter eat—dat dere's mah hidin' place. Nobody can't see yo'all, nobody can't fin' yo' dere!"

While he talked and the others snatched their half dried things from before the fire, the old darky was clearing the table of dishes. He flung the remains of the meal onto the blazing logs and scooping up the cups and plates, stacked them, dirty as they were, on a shelf.

Dorothy and Bill ran into the back room and scrambled up to the crossbeams. As they crawled along the boards which were laid close together in threes, they saw

Uncle Abe light an ancient corncob, then pick up a tattered newspaper and sit down by the fire. No more had they laid themselves flat on their airy perch with their bundles of damp clothing, than there came a pounding on the cabin door.

"Who dat?" called out Ol' Man River without moving from his chair.

"Open up, do you hear, River? I want to speak to you," barked a voice from out the night.

"Yaas, suh—comin'!"

Peering through the cracks between the boards, his guests saw him rise slowly and shuffle to the door. Stretched out over the little bed chamber, with their heads close to the partition, they had an unobstructed view of the lighted room beyond. As the boards were laid over the middle of both rooms and ran nearly the length of the cabin, they realized with satisfaction that unless someone stood close to the side wall, it would be impossible to spy them out. Uncle Abe's oil lamp sent its gleams but a few feet, and the rest of the room and the crossbeams lay in deep shadow which was an added protection to the hidden two.

Ol' Man River drew the bolt and swung open the door.

"Walk right in, Marse Joyce," they heard him say. And without waiting for a reply, he hobbled painfully back to his chair before the hearth.

Three men stamped into the cabin and banged the door shut on the storm.

"You're keeping late hours, River," the leader of the party snapped out without preamble.

From the tones of his voice, Dorothy and Bill knew him to be the same man who had spoken to them in the valley meadow, and who Bill had downed with the gasoline tin. He was a short, stocky person with a bulldog face and a scrubby toothbrush moustache. He and his companions looked tired and angry. They were also very wet.

The speaker walked over to the fire, leaving a track of little pools across the floor. Putting his hands over the blaze, he scowled down at Uncle Abe.

"Well," he contended disagreeably, "I

said you were up late. Answer me, can't you?"

"So yo' say, Marse Joyce. So yo' say."

Uncle Abe continued to gaze unconcernedly into the fire as though he had no idea the heavy set man was becoming angrier by the minute.

"You black whelp!" he thundered. "What do you mean by bandying words with me?"

Uncle Abe remained silent.

"Are you deaf?" cried Joyce. "Tell me what you're sitting up for!"

"I'se takin' a warm, suh."

"Taking a—*warm?*"

"Yaas, suh. I'se a mis'ry in der feet—rhumytizzem. Can't sleep nohow. So I sets an' reads de paper by de fire—an' takes a warm."

"Oh, you do, do you?"

"Yaas, suh, I sho' do."

"Don't answer me back that way, do you hear?"

The old darky continued to puff calmly on his corncob.

Mr. Joyce thrust his hands in his pockets

and glowered at him. His companions stood silently by, watching Uncle Abe.

"Where are your visitors?" he asked suddenly.

Bill released the safety-catch on his automatic.

Uncle Abe puffed steadily on his pipe, but said nothing.

"Answer me! Where are they?" snarled John J. Joyce.

"Yaas, suh!" The old darky removed the corncob from his mouth and looked up at his late employer.

"Well, why don't you speak?"

"Kase yo' done tell me not ter answer a while back."

"I tell you to answer me now." Mr. Joyce glared threateningly into his face. "Are you just stubborn, or in your dotage? *Where are your visitors?*"

The old man spat with great precision on to a glowing cinder. "Dey right hyar, Marse Joyce," he said.

"Right here? Where?"

"Hyar in dis room, suh. All three o' yo'."

"Say, are you crazy, or am I?" Joyce flung at him.

"No, suh, I ain' crazy," returned the old man, and Joyce's companions broke into a roar of laughter at this none too subtle gibe.

John J. Joyce turned on them furiously.

"Shut up, you two! Go into that back room and pull them out!"

Still guffawing, the men disappeared through the doorway in the partition.

"Nobody in here!" a voice sang out after a moment.

Joyce looked bewildered. Then he picked up the lamp, walked to the open door and looked into the room.

"Yank that bed apart!" he ordered.

The two lying on the boards above his head heard the men dragging the evergreen boughs off the couch. Joyce said not a word when their search was ended, but turned on his heel and returned to the front room, followed by his henchmen.

"Didn't think yo'd fin' nobody," remarked Uncle Abe mildly, "If yo' had, I'd sho' bin supprised!"

"So you'd been surprised, eh?"

John J. Joyce had an unpleasant way of repeating words. Now he stood over the old man belligerently.

"Yaas, suh," replied Uncle Abe with an unconcern he probably did not feel. "I could o' tol' yo' dat dey's nobody in dere. Who yo' all a-lookin' fo'?"

"What business is that of yours?"

The old man remained silent.

"If you must know," snarled Joyce, "we're looking for a young fellow and a girl."

"What dey doin' uphyar in de woods at dis time o' night?"

"Tryin' to get away from us, I guess," said one of the men.

"You keep your trap shut, Feather-stone," barked Joyce. "I'm not paying you to talk. This is my show, not yours."

"Well, if you talk that way, you can run it by yourself. I'm not your slave. Keep a civil tongue in your head, Joyce—or I'll go back to the car—and go right now."

"That goes with me, too," broke in the second man gruffly. "What d'you take us for—a pair of fools? I wasn't hired to do a marathon the length and breadth of the forest on a soakin' wet night. Those kids ain't here—let's go!"

"Oh, is that so? Well now you've had your say, and you'll go—when I get good and ready," sneered Joyce in his disagreeable, domineering voice.

"But what's the use of hangin' round?" argued the first man. "I'm tired and I'm hungry and I'm soaked to the skin—"

"And if I say the word to certain parties, the two of you will be taking a longer journey," snapped their employer, "—a little trip up the river that ends in a chair—a red hot one. Shut up, both of you."

He turned to Uncle Abe again. "Come, River—out with it," he commanded. "Where have that boy and girl gone to?"

"How should I know?" Uncle Abe knocked his pipe out on the hearth. "What fo' yo'all chasin' dese hyar chillun in de woods?"

"That's my business. There are fresh tracks leading along the trail right up to your door."

"Dat may be, suh. Day may be. I ain't sayin' dey isn't, Marse Joyce." He wagged his head solemnly. "I wuz out myse'f e'rlier in de evenin'."

"Huh! You wouldn't leave two sets of tracks!"

"Yaas, suh, Marse Joyce—goin' an' comin'."

Dorothy, from her perch above, smiled at the old darky's astuteness. Their tracks were on the trail, of course, for those who followed to read; but the rain had long ago blurred the outlines. Their pursuers could not know in which direction the footprints led.

"So you think it was your tracks we followed?"

John J. Joyce continued to speak in the harsh, bullying tone that made Dorothy want to kick him. She realized, nevertheless, that the old darky's last statement was proving a serious facer to his inquisitor.

"I ain't a-gwine ter say jes' dat," returned Uncle Abe. "All I knows is dat I made tracks on de trail. If dey's more'n two pair, dey ain't mine."

"What trails were you on?" came the sudden question, and Dorothy tingled with excitement as Uncle Abe hesitated.

"Lemme see, suh—why, I wuz down de Spy Rock Trail, an' de Cross Trail. And den I wuz 'long de Overlook and de Raven Rock Trails—"

"A nice long walk you had on a wet night," sneered the white man.

Uncle Abe was imperturbable. "Yaas, suh."

"I don't believe a word of it."

"Dat yo' priv-lige, Marse Joyce."

"Well, it doesn't sound likely to me, especially when you say you've rheumatism in your feet."

"I'se gotter eat, suh."

"What's that got to do with it? There are no stores on these trails. What do you pretend you were doing, anyway?"

Ol' Man River chuckled gently. "Bait in' traps."

"Catch anything?" Joyce sneered. "I don't suppose you did."

"Den you's a mighty bad 'sposer, suh. Kaze I done cotch dat der rabbit yonder!"

Following the direction of his pointed finger, Dorothy saw for the first time that a large jackrabbit hung from a crossbeam in a corner.

"It's no go, Joyce," broke in one of the henchmen. "This nigger doesn't know where those kids are. Let's beat it."

Joyce, who had unbuttoned his coat, fastened it up again.

"For once you're right," he admitted truculently. "It's time we got back to the car. That pair have holed in for the night somewhere else. We'll watch the reservation entrances in the morning."

"Good night, suh, and a pleasant walk!"

Dorothy had hard work to repress her laughter. She loved this spunky old negro.

Joyce turned angrily upon him. "You keep a civil tongue in your face, River!" he menaced. "In the first place, this is a state preserve, and poaching is severely punished; and secondly, you have no right to be squatting in this shelter, I—"

"Pick on someone your size, Joyce," advised the man who had spoken before. "This old nigger ain't doin' you nor anyone else any harm. Leave him alone."

"It's two to one, Joyce. Come on!" said the other.

For a moment Dorothy thought there would be a row. Joyce looked as though he would burst with rage. But evidently thinking better of it, he turned his back to the fire and strode over to the door. Without another word, he opened it and disappeared into the black night.

He was followed immediately by the two men. The one who had spoken for Abe swung round in the doorway.

"I know you're a good hearted old liar, Uncle," he whispered. "And if you think a minute you'll know why I know it! Don't blame you. Joyce has a nasty temper and no matter where those kids are, we'll round 'em up in the morning, anyway. Good night!"

"'Night," returned Ol' Man River. "Pleasant walk, suh!"

"Yep. The joke's on us," grinned the other and shut the door behind him.

Bill and Dorothy were about to move from their cramped positions when they saw the old man raise a finger to his lips in warning as apparently he studied the glowing embers of the fire.

The door suddenly opened and the same man stuck his head in.

"You're a sly old fox," he said. "I know you've got those kids hidden somewhere. Maybe they're listening for all I know, and I can tell you, Uncle, they are getting a rotten deal. Joyce calls me Featherstone. Here's my card. Give it to them. G'd-night."

A bit of white pasteboard fluttered to the floor as the door slammed.

Uncle Abe got stiffly off his chair, shuffled over to the door and sent the bolt home. Then he picked up the card.

Bill pushed the pile of damp clothing off the boards, then swung himself down to the floor. Dorothy was beside him as he turned to catch her.

"Uncle Abe," she said, taking the old man's hand, "you are kind and you're good, and you are very, very brave. Bill and I can never properly thank you for all you've done for us tonight."

"Say no mo' 'bout it," protested Uncle Abe, when Bill put his hand on his shoulder.

"Look here, Uncle Abe," he broke in, "you're one of the grandest guys I know. Some day perhaps we can even up things a bit. You ran a big risk for us, you know."

The old man smiled and blinked at them for a moment. "Then, yo'all must be sleepy—I sho' is. You kin take the back room if you will, Missy. Marse Bill an' me's gwine ter hit de hay in here."

"Who was that man, Uncle Abe?" asked Dorothy, stifling a yawn with the palm of her hand. "What did his card say, I mean?"

"Spec' he's a deteckative, Missy. De card say 'Michael Michaels, Private Inquiry Agent'."

"Evidently he's got his eye on Joyce," summed up Bill. "Wonder who he's working for?"

"What interests me more just now," said Dorothy, "is how Mister Michael Michaels knew we were hidden here."

The old man chuckled.

"He's sho' 'nuf a smart man, Missy. It

wuz de tracks on de trail. He know'd I done never make dem tracks. He know'd dey wan't nobody else's but yourn."

"How come, uncle?" asked Bill.

"Dat jackrabbit a-hangin' yonder done it, suh."

"But what's that rabbit got to do with our tracks?"

"Marse Michaels, he must o' touched dat bunny. Den he know'd it wan't never trapped today. Dat bunny's stiff ez er hick'ry log!"

Dorothy and Bill burst into laughter.

"Bet you were scared silly for fear Joyce might examine it and realize that you hadn't been out tonight!" said Bill.

"Dat's right, sho' nuf, Marse Bill."

"You know, Mr. Michaels may be a big help to us," remarked Dorothy, yawning unashamedly in their faces this time. "Well, I just can't hold my head up any longer. Good night, both of you."

"Good night," returned Bill and Uncle Abe in unison.

Dorothy took herself off to the back room and bed.

Chapter XIII

THE WAY OUT

The gray light of early morning crept into Shelter No. 6 through the open shutters. It brought to view two forms rolled in blankets, sleeping soundly before the dying embers of last night's woodfire. In the back room, Dorothy was curled up on the fragrant bed of evergreens, deep in a dreamless slumber. The storm of the evening was gone, leaving in its place a fine, steady drizzle. The air was chill and damp. It bade fair to be another unpleasant day.

The hands of a battered alarm clock that stood on the chimney shelf marked quarter to eight, but the sleepers were motionless. Then suddenly Uncle Abe sat up and knuckled the sleep from his eyes.

"Lordy, Lordy!" he grumbled, catching sight of the clock. "Dose chillun wuz ter git 'way early an' dis hyer nigger sleepin'

lak de daid. I speck de young Missy an'
Marse Bill need der sleep—an' we'll fool
Marse Joyce jus' de same."

He got stiffly to his feet, stretched his
ancient arms above his head and set about
building up the fire.

Presently Bill opened his eyes and
yawned. Then he threw off his blanket,
sat up and sniffed.

"Bacon—eggs—coffee," he murmured.
"Good morning, Uncle, you sure are an
A1. up to the minute chef!"

Hovering over a sizzling frying pan,
the old man turned his head and smiled at
Bill.

"Mornin', Marse Bill. Yaas, suh, I
'low dat eatin' brekfus' an' gettin' it, too, is
de bes' fashion what is."

"You said it," grinned Bill. "Say, I
guess we all overslept! Well, no use cross-
ing our bridges 'til we come to 'em. Any
place in this hotel where I can wash and
slick up a bit, Uncle?"

"Sho' is, suh. De soap an' de towel an'
de bucket an' de basin is over yonder by
de do'. When yo'alls done wid dem, p'raps

yo'll wake de young missy, an' carry de bucket in yonder?"

"Sure will," returned Bill, "but I'll wake her up first."

He went to the door in the partition and banged his fist on the panels.

"First call for breakfast in the dining car ahead—"

"Ummm—" responded a sleepy voice from the back room.

"Time to get up, Dorothy. Hop to it, kid!"

"I'm awake!" called back that young lady.

"O.K. When you're ready, there'll be a pail of water outside your door."

"Thanks. Be with you in a jiffy."

Bill crossed the room, sloshed water into the tin basin and carried the pail back. While he was immersed in his morning ablutions Dorothy's door opened and her hand withdrew the pail.

Bill had no more than taken a seat at the table, when she put in her appearance. Dressed in the overalls, flannel shirt and heavy wool socks of the night before, she looked particularly bright and cheerful.

"Morning, everybody!" she smiled. "That bed of yours, Uncle Abe, is the most comfortable one I ever slept on. Too bad I had to turn you out of it."

"Reckon neither Marse Bill ner me knowed what we wuz a-sleepin' on, Missy. I sho' wuz daid ter ebbryt'ing all night long. De flo' ain't discomfertubble, when yo' knows how ter lay on it."

"I'm kind of stiff," admitted Bill. "But I feel fifty million per cent better. Bet I never moved from the time I turned in until the smell of breakfast woke me up."

"My!" exclaimed Dorothy, peeking into the frying pan. "Where did all these swell eggs come from, Uncle?"

The old darky chuckled.

"Dat's one o' de two things a white pusson mus'nt never ask no color'd pusson, Missy."

"And what's the other?" Dorothy inquired with twinkling eyes.

"Where a nigger gits his chickens."

All three of them laughed this time and sat down to breakfast.

During the meal there was little conversation. Both Dorothy and Bill were frankly hungry and each was silently puzzling a way out of their predicament. Uncle Abe, always affable, nevertheless, rarely if ever volunteered advice unless called upon. In his mind, to do otherwise would have been a breach of good manners.

Bill drained his second cup of coffee and met Dorothy's look.

"Got any ideas?" he asked her.

She shook her head and pushed her chair back from the table. "No, I haven't," she confessed gravely. "But if I'm any judge of bad character, Mr. John J. Joyce will keep his promise. Too bad we slept so long."

"Maybe," said Bill. "But without that good rest, we'd have been dead ones today. The tough part of it is that Joyce's men will be posted at all the reservation entrances now—"

"And on the trails around this shelter."

"Very likely. If we could ditch those guys and hike over to a road, we might get a lift out in somebody's car. Lots of people drive in here on Sundays."

"Not in weather like this, Bill. No, even if we did persuade someone to give us a lift, we'd be soon seen and stopped."

Bill suddenly brought his fist down upon the table.

"We're a pair of idiots," he declared. "Joyce's men won't stop us. They'll be looking for Stoker Conway and a girl. Keep those clothes on you're wearing, and with my old hat, all they'll see is a couple of fellows on a tramp. Nobody'd take me for George Conway. Why, we've got nothing to worry about!"

"That's where I differ with you. We most certainly have plenty to worry us."

"But how come, Dorothy?"

"How do we know that friend Joyce hasn't got hold of Stoker and possibly Terry, too?"

"Then—if he has, he won't want us."

"Oh, yes, he will. You can bet your boots, Mr. Joyce isn't letting anyone go whom he may think was mixed up in last night's affair."

Bill looked surprised. "But Joyce can't go on kidnapping people," he argued. "Or rather he can't keep on trying to kidnap the whole bunch who were in Stoker's house last night, and then hold them indefinitely. Even if he caught us all, he couldn't hold us long."

"Long enough to get what he thinks Stoker has got—and make his getaway, if necessary. At least that's how I figure it. If he catches any of us we're not likely to come in personal contact with him. He's too smart to give himself away like that."

"Possibly you're right. But if he did catch any of us, he'd soon find out that Stoker and the rest of the bunch know less about this mysterious something he's after than he does himself!"

Dorothy smiled. "Rather involved, but I think I fathom your meaning. You seem to forget, Bill, that when Betty and I butted into this thing up at the Conway house, a couple of strong-arm men were starting to heat a poker. I don't think Mr. Joyce's hospitality will prove a pleasant experience if we are caught by him or his men."

"Well, we've got to get off this reservation—how are we going to do it?"

"Blest if I know," she admitted candidly. "But we've just got to find a way. And look here, Bill—I know you think I'm all steamed up over a trifle—but I honestly believe that whatever Joyce is trying to steal from Stoker is so enormously valuable that he's determined to risk pretty nearly everything short of murder to gain possession of it!"

"I wouldn't put murder past him, either," said Bill.

"His actions prove he's in deadly earnest," Dorothy went on, and then turned to Ol' Man River, who was peacefully puffing his pipe. "You've heard what we were saying, Uncle Abe. Have you any suggestions to give us?"

That ancient colored gentleman removed the corncob from between his teeth and pursed his lips. "Waal, yaas, m'am. I reckon Marse Johnson is de answer to yo' question," he said thoughtfully.

"Oh, he's the reservation superintendent—you're right, Uncle Abe—he can do it if anyone can. Why didn't we think of him before?"

"Dat am so, Missy. Der ain't a-gwine nobody ter stop yo'all long wid Marse Johnson."

"That's a great idea, Uncle," applauded Bill. "The super's house is right across the reservation from here, if I recall rightly?"

"Yaas, suh, it am. Right down yonder where de Boutonville road come out far side ob de reservation t'ard Cross River."

"Think you could pilot us down there and give those guys in the woods the miss?"

"I speck dese men ain't gwine ter git familious wid us if yo' foller Ol' Man River. I'se boun' we-all sho' give 'em de bestes' game er hide an' seek dey ez ever had. It ain't a-gwine be easy, Marse Bill. But I'll git yo'all down yonder and den you kin carry de young Missy home in a kyar. Marse Johnson, he's got three auto-merbiles."

"I hope it'll be as easy as you say," grinned Bill, amused by the old man's earnestness. "I'll make a bundle of Miss

Dorothy's clothes and then the best thing we can do is to get started."

"I'se got a pair er sneakers dat you kin wear, Missy," Uncle Abe announced. "Dey ain't no count nohow, but dey's got sol's an' dat sho' am better dan walkin' in dose socks."

"Thanks a lot, Uncle, you're such a grand help to us—" She smiled at the old man and he fairly beamed. "I'll love wearing them. But first of all, we'll heat some water and wash dishes. Don't look so annoyed, Bill. We've got plenty of time, now, and there's nothing more slovenly than letting the dishes go after a meal. We did it because we had to last night, but I intend to leave Uncle Abe's cabin just as spick and span as we found it. You fetch some water and heat it while Uncle Abe scrapes the plates. In the meantime I'll straighten up the back room and sweep out the house."

Dorothy was as good as her word. By the time the dish water was hot, her bed had been made, the cabin swept and generally put to rights. Then she brought out the dishpan and washed both the supper and breakfast dishes while Bill and Uncle Abe dried them.

"Some swell housekeeper," said Bill to Uncle Abe with a grimace, "and she knows how to make the men folks work, too!"

"An' dat am ez it should be," declared the old darky solemnly. "De Good Book say, 'what am food fo' de goose am good eatin' fo' de gander' . . ."

"I don't know whether that's a compliment, or not, Uncle," laughed Dorothy. "But you see, it didn't take long, and I feel better knowing everything's clean."

"Is your ladyship ready to go now?" asked Bill.

"Quite ready—thank you so much."

"Then let's shove off. What you said about Stoker and Terry a while ago has got me worried, I must admit. I want to get to a telephone just as soon as possible."

Uncle Abe left the cabin first. After scouting about in the cold drizzle for a few minutes, he came back and declared that the way was clear.

"I gen'rally goes 'long Overlook Trail an' down de Cross River Road ter git er

Marse Johnson's house," explained the old man, once they were outside the cabin.

"But dis mornin' we ain't gwine dataway—t'aint safe. Yo' all stick close behin' Ol' Man River, an' sing out ef he's a-travelin' too fast. Dis ain't no easy trail we'se takin'."

He struck directly into the woods and for the next hour Dorothy never even sighted a path. She soon found out that when Uncle Abe described this as 'no easy trail,' he was telling the unvarnished truth. Dorothy was no Alice-sit-by-the-fire. She had been on some stiff hikes before this, but the ancient negro led them up hill and down dale, through the tangled undergrowth or virgin forest dripping wet with rain. And he led them through this wilderness of trees and rocks at a perfectly amazing rate of speed. Until Dorothy caught her second wind, she was hard put to keep up.

If Joyce had men out, they never saw them. In fact, except for an occasional bird or small forest animal scuttling away in their advance, they neither saw nor heard any living thing. Eventually they climbed the steep side of a wooded ridge and stopped.

Below them, through the trees Dorothy made out woodland meadows, stretching down to a road which ran along their side of the valley. Lower down and paralleling the highway, a winding river ran down the vale. Lying in broad fields near the river to their left was a large farm house and barns.

"Cross River Road, Cross River, and Marse Johnson's house," announced Uncle Abe, using a hand and forearm for a pointer. "Dat highway yonder what runs inter de Cross River Road near de house ez de Honey Holler Road. Right dar am de Cross River entrance, an' right dar ez 'zackly de place whar ol' man Joyce's gang am hangin' out."

"It's going to be a job to get down there without being seen," remarked Bill.

"Der ain't nobody gwine ter see us," protested the old darky, "kaze soon ex we git ter der open, you an' me an' Missy am gwine ter ben' down low an' hug de far side er de stone fences. But we'alls stayed hyar confabbin' long 'nuf. Got ter git goin' ag'in.''

He moved off down the slope, the others following. By dint of doing exactly as he advised, fifteen minutes later found them ringing Mr. Johnson's doorbell.

"Dese young people am fren's er mine, Miz Johnson," Uncle Abe told the motherly person who opened the door.

"Step right in," she invited with a smile. "Lands sakes, you're drippin' wet. Come in by the kitchen range and get dried out. You must be perishin'—"

"Thanks. May I use your telephone?" inquired Bill as he spied a wall instrument in the hall.

"Of course you can," beamed Mrs. Johnson. "There's a book on the table there."

"Thank you, I know the number."

"Going to call up Stoker?" asked Dorothy in a low tone.

"Yes. You and Uncle Abe go into the kitchen and get warm. I'll be with you in a minute or two."

But it was not until a good five minutes later that Bill put in his appearance.

"Everything all right?" demanded Dorothy from her seat on a kitchen chair close to the coal range.

"I'm afraid not," Bill looked worried. "They don't answer the phone."

Chapter XIV

THE LION'S DEN

"No answer at all?" Dorothy inquired anxiously.

"That's what I said." Bill's tone was a bit gruff. He walked over to the range and warmed his hands at the glowing coals.

"What I mean is, could you hear the bell ring in Stoker's house?"

"Oh, yes, the bell rang. But nobody came to the phone."

"That's what I wanted to know."

"Why? I can't see that the ringing of the phone bell makes any difference—"

"All the difference," declared Dorothy. "Never mind why, now. I've just told Mrs. Johnson that I had to park *Wispy* on the other side of the reservation last night, and that some men over there were very disagreeable and we were forced to accept Uncle Abe's hospitality for the night."

"We think a heap of Uncle Abe on the reservation," affirmed the superintendent's wife. "And don't you worry about your airplane, Miss Dixon. We'll see that it don't come to no harm. My husband had to drive over to Katonah this morning, but I'll get Sam Watson on the job. He's in the office right now. Sam!" she called, "come in here."

A stalwart, broad-shouldered young man walked into the kitchen. His natty uniform marked him a member of the Reservation force.

"Did you want something, Mrs. Johnson?"

"This is Miss Dorothy Dixon of New Canaan, and Mr.—" she hesitated.

"Bolton—Bill Bolton," supplied that young man.

"The flyers!" Guard Watson's honest face wore a broad grin. "Heard about you both—who hasn't? Pleased to meet you, I'm sure." He shook hands with them and nodded to Uncle Abe.

"It's like this, Sam," explained Mrs. Johnson. "Miss Dixon run out of gas last night and her airplane is down to the wood-lot just below Raven Rocks in the Stone Hill River valley. Get Eddie, that's his beat anyway, and keep an eye on the airplane until these young folks pick it up this afternoon. They had trouble with some tramps over there last evenin' and put up to Uncle Abe's for the night. Pass the word on to the rest of the boys about them dead beats that's botherin' people on the Reservation, will you?"

"I sure will, Mrs. Johnson. If they're still around, we'll run 'em off quicker'n greased lightning."

"You're very good," smiled Dorothy. "We saw a couple of suspicious characters hanging round the Cross River entrance when we came over here to headquarters just now."

"I'll rout 'em out," Sam Watson promised. "If they kick up a fuss they'll put in thirty days behind the bars. Well, I must be hoppin' it. Glad to have met you folks, I'm sure. So long, everybody!"

With a stiff salute and a broad smile he was gone. They heard him tramp down the hall and then the front door slammed.

"Checkmate to J. J. J.," murmured Bill.

Dorothy played chess with her father—"Not checkmate—check," she corrected. "By the way, Mrs. Johnson, I wonder if we can trespass on your good humor still further?"

"Land's sakes alive! I haven't done nothing for you yet!" The superintendent's wife was busy with hot water and a teapot.

"Do you happen to have an extra car that we could borrow for a few hours?"

"Why, sure I have, my dear. But there's no hurry about your leavin', is there? A cup of tea, now, to warm you up and some of these nice crisp crullers I made yesterday? Then I'll get you and Mr. Bolton some dry things to put on and after dinner you can take the car and ride home. How'll that be?"

Dorothy laughed and shook her head. "You're awfully kind, really, Mrs. Johnson, but we can't stay. We've got an appointment that just can't be broken."

"But your wet clothes, Miss Dixon?"

"Thanks for your offer, but we aren't so wet now. I will have a cup of tea if I may, although we only finished breakfast a little while ago."

"And don't forget those crisp crullers," protested Bill with a grin. "I certainly do love homemade crullers, ma'am."

"An' dey ain't nuffin' better 'an de ones Miz Johnson makes," chuckled Uncle Abe. "I'se tasted 'em befo' an' dis hyar nigger knows!"

Mrs. Johnson beamed delightedly.

"Even if I do say so who shouldn't," she remarked modestly, "this batch came out pretty good. But are you sure I can't tempt you to stay for Sunday dinner? We're having fish chowder, chicken fricassee, with dumplin's, and a pumpkin pie!"

"You sure do make my mouth water," groaned Bill. "I only wish we could stop, and meet your husband, Mrs. Johnson. If you'll keep the invitation open, we'd love to take advantage of it some other time."

The good lady passed them their tea and a plate heaped with golden brown crullers.

"We'll make it next Sunday noon then. Our children are all married, with homes of their own. Mr. Johnson and I miss not having young folks round the house. It'll make it seem like the good old times again, if you come. Don't forget now, next Sunday."

"We'll be here with bells on, Mrs. Johnson," promised Bill.

"And we'll try not to look like a couple of tramps then," added Dorothy.

"You'll always be welcome, no matter what you wear," declared their hostess. "I'll make another pumpkin pie for you."

They chatted for ten minutes or so and then bade Mrs. Johnson goodbye.

"Uncle Abe will take you out to the garage," she said in parting. "Take the Buick. You'll need a closed car on a day like this."

When the kitchen door had shut out the smiling, motherly figure, and they were following the old darky along the drive, Dorothy turned to Bill.

"And they say that New Englanders are not hospitable! Why, they're the most hos-

pitable people in America if you really
know them!"

"Country people, no matter what part of
the United States they live in, are generally
friendly. Living in cities, where your next
door neighbor is a stranger, makes a person suspicious. But I've found that most
honest-to-goodness Americans will do a
lot for a person in trouble."

"Dere's de kyar, Missy," Uncle Abe interrupted apologetically. "Reckon dis
hyar ol' nigger'll wish yo' all goodbye an'
mo' comferble beds ternight."

Dorothy caught the old fellow's hand
and held it between her own.

"Uncle Abe," she said, looking straight
into his shining eyes, "do you really like
living up there in the woods, all by yourself?"

"Waal, dis nigger ain't used ter much,
Missy," he said slowly, "an' de cabin am a
heap better 'an a barn er no roof atall. But,
it sho' do get mighty lonesome, 'times."

"I bet it does. How would you like to
live in quarters over our garage and work
for my father? He was saying only a day

or so ago that what with driving the cars
and all Arthur has too much to do around
the place. We need a gardener and gen-
eral handy man. The job is yours if you'll
take it—and I don't mind saying I'll feel
badly if you don't."

Ol' Man River winked back the tears
with a brave effort, although the little
wrinkles at the corners of his mouth puck-
ered in a smile.

"Yo' sho' is good ter dis hyar nigger,
Missy!"

"And you want to come? I won't take
no for an answer—"

"It do me good fer ter hear you sesso,
Missy. Kaze yo' sho' is de qual'ty and dis
hyar ol' nigger never done had no real
fambly 'time he come No'th."

Bill winked at Uncle Abe.

"And if that nocount Dixon family don't
treat you right, you come right across the
road to my house."

"Spect I'll git 'long tollerbul well on
Miss Dor'thy's side," he chuckled.

"Well, what's the good word now,
Dorothy?" Bill motioned toward the

Buick. "It's about time we beat it over to Stoker's, don't you think?"

"I do think," returned Dorothy. "And that's why we aren't going over there."

"But surely—"

"But nothing. The boys aren't there or they'd have answered the phone. If you hadn't heard the bell ring we could be fairly sure the wire was cut and that they were holding the house in a state of siege, so to speak. Now we know they aren't there." Bill did not seem impressed.

"If that line of reasoning is logical, I'm as cold on the right answer as a water tank in winter. How do you know Joyce's men haven't got them tied up in the house?"

"Because at this stage of the game, Joyce would hardly do that and leave them there for their friends to find. And if his men were still in the house, they'd be sure to answer the telephone. You and Uncle Abe get right into that Buick now. We are going to take a run up to Mr. John J. Joyce's place."

Bill did not attempt to hide his astonishment.

"Gee, whiz, Dorothy—you've got a whale of a lot of nerve!"

Dorothy shrugged and looked steadily at Bill. "Well, are you game?"

For answer he followed her into the car.

"Pretty much like jumping feet first into the lion's den," he commented, "but considering your middle name is Daniel, or ought to be, I dare say we'll have a roaring good time of it!"

"Stop talking jazz, Bill. How about you, Uncle Abe?"

The old man already lounged back on the rear seat.

"Reverse dis hyar injine inter de drive, Miss Dor'thy—an' when yo'all turned round I'se gwine ter show yo' where we'se a-gwine."

Dorothy, smiling over the steering wheel, backed out of the garage and got the Buick headed toward the road.

"Well, Uncle?" she prompted.

"D'reckly in front of us, way over yonder on de far hill ez er big house."

"The white one in the trees?" asked Bill.

"Yaas, suh, de only one any pusson kin

see from hyar. Dat am Hilltop, Marse Conway's ol' place."

"Where Mr. Lewis lives now!"

"Eggzackly so, ma'am. Marse Joyce's place ez jus' back er yonder."

"Bet he calls it, 'The Den,'" said Bill.

Uncle Abe cackled, "No, suh, Marse Bill—hee-hee—dat house done called 'Nearma'."

"Near ma?" repeated Dorothy in a puzzled tone. "There are some queer Indian names in this part of the country, but that's a new one on me."

"'Tain't Injun, Missy. Dat dere hones' ter goodness 'Merican. Marse Joyce's ol' Ma uster lib cross de ridgeroad. Dat how he come ter name de house 'Near Ma'."

"That old scurmudgeon! I don't believe it!" cried Bill in an explosion of laughter.

"Dat am de spittin' trufe, Marse Bill. De ol' lady am daid, but he still call de place Nearma jus' de same."

"How do we get to it, Uncle?" Dorothy asked after a moment.

"Run out de entrance till we come ter de turnpike, Missy. Den right, long dat road to Cross River. From de village yonder we follers de road ter Lake Waccabuc, but we don't hafter travel dat far."

"Good enough." The car swung round the side of the house and into the road. "I guess Sam got rid of the Watchers by the Gate—there's nobody at the entrance."

They swept into the highroad and on through the pre-revolutionary hamlet of Cross River. Half a mile further, as they were speeding along the top of a wooded ridge, Uncle Abe spoke again.

"Dat stone fence long de road ter de right b'long ter Hilltop," he pointed out. "De house am set way back from de road behin' de trees. Round de bend ahead yo'-all gwine ter see 'nother higher wall, dat starts by three white birches. Yonder am where Marse Joyce's land begins."

"And what's on the farther side of the Joyce property?"

"Dere ain't nuffin, Missy, 'cept jes' mo' dese hyar woods."

"Fine! And I suppose, after being up here for nearly ten years, you can find your way about in those woods?"

"Sho' can, Missy. Ef dere's er rabbit hole dis nigger a' missed in dem woods, I wanter know."

"Better and better. You're a marvelous help, Uncle Abe."

"What do you plan to do? Park the car near the road, hike back through the woods and cut over toward the house from that side?" Bill was not enthusiastic.

"Just about that."

"And when you sight the historic mansion?"

"I'm going into the house."

"Oh, yes, you are . . ."

"Oh, yes, I am!"

"And how do you expect to do that without being nabbed right off the bat?"

"Last night you told me I asked too many questions, Bill. And Uncle Abe says 'what's food for the goose is swell eating for the gander . . .'!"

Chapter XV

IN THE TOILS

"Ef yo'll pahdon my sayin' so, Miss Do'thy," volunteered Uncle Abe as the car was run into the underbrush beyond the Nearma wall and parked behind a clump of scrub oak and evergreens, "I 'lows as how it sho' would er bin better ter 'proach de house from de odder side. We could er travelled down Marse Lewis' place and come in dat-a-way. Dere's mo' lan'-scapin' on dat side."

"Thanks for the suggestion, Uncle." Dorothy locked the ignition. "But I think we'll keep just as far away from Mr. Lewis' property as we can, for the present."

"Do you think he really is mixed up with J. J. J. in this business?" Bill asked her.

"Can't say—it certainly looks like it—and we'll take no unnecessary chances."

"How about the chances we'll take in breaking into Nearma?"

"I said unnecessary! Anyway, I'm the one that's going in there."

"But look here, Dorothy! Do you think I'm going to let you walk into that place alone?"

"Not alone, old dear. Uncle Abe is coming with me."

"Oh, is he? And what am I to do while you're in the house mixing it up with those thugs? Do you expect me to stick out here with the car and see that somebody doesn't steal the tires?"

Dorothy looked amused. Bill was annoyed with her and she did not blame him. "You'll have plenty to do, Bill." She gave his shoulder a good-natured pat and sprang out of the car.

"Come on, both of you. I'll explain my plan as we go. Lead the way, Uncle Abe. I want to get to the kitchen door without being seen from the house if possible."

Uncle Abe got out of the car. Bill was already beside her.

"Yo'all foller Ol' Man River!" said the ancient darky and led into the woods away from the road.

"Well, what's the dope?" Bill's tone was less exasperated now, and side by side they swung in behind the old man.

Dorothy took his arm. "I guess you think I'm a brainless idiot," she began, "with all my wild schemes—"

"Well, I don't quite see your idea in going in there alone—but it's your show, so go ahead and explain."

"Attaboy! Now this is the point. I want to do some scouting inside and I'll need you to cover me as it were. Uncle Abe knows Joyce's servants. And Mr. Joyce is looking for you and me. Well, don't you see, if Uncle Abe brings a stray *boy* into the kitchen for a bite to eat, it won't seem anything out of the way. In these clothes, I'll never be taken for a girl."

"But you won't stay in the kitchen—I know you!" Bill was not quite convinced.

"Perhaps not—what I do inside will depend on circumstances as I find 'em."

"Humph! And what is my important work to consist of?"

"I want you to watch this side of the house. If I need you, I'll open a window and wave. If it happens to be a window on the ground floor, you can get in that way. If I open a second story window, come in through the kitchen. You've got a gun—that ought to be a help."

"But—suppose you aren't able to get to a window?"

"Oh, then wait half an hour; when the time's up run down to Cross River in the car and phone the state police and get them up here just as soon as possible."

"Why not get them up here now?"

"Because we really haven't got anything to go on. Chances are they wouldn't come and I want to be able to pin something good and definite on Mr. John J. Joyce before we get the police on the job."

Bill seemed impressed by her reasoning. "I guess you're right. If Stoker and Terry are in Nearma and we can prove it, J. J. J. will have a nice little charge of kidnapping to face."

"And I want to get him for grand larceny and conspiracy as well," she returned. "That may sound ambitious, but I want to land that gentleman and his friends on a bunch of counts that will send them to Sing Sing for a very, very long time."

"You and me both. I don't know what Joyce's plans are, but after listening to his bark last night, I'll bet they're something pretty rotten. Hello!—There's Uncle Abe beckoning."

They caught up with the old darky who was peering through the woods to their right.

"Yonder's de stone fence, Missy," he announced, "an' beyon' am Marse Joyce's prop'ty. De house am 'bout fifty yards from de fence."

"Good. Bill, you go ahead and lay low behind some of the bushes near the house. Uncle Abe and I will be along in a minute."

"Aye, aye, skipper. Take care of yourself."

With a wave of his hand he climbed the low stone wall and disappeared into the shrubbery on the Joyce grounds.

Dorothy turned to Ol' Man River. "I suppose you know the cook over there, Uncle?"

"Oh, yaas, ma'am. Liza an' me's bin frien's fer ten years."

"That's fine. Now listen to what I say, because you've got your part to play in this affair and there mustn't be any slipup."

For several minutes she talked earnestly to the old negro.

"Is that all clear?" she ended presently.

"Yaas, missy. I'll do what yo'all tells me to—but I ain't 'zackly hankerin' fer you to do all dis."

Dorothy laughed. "Neither am I, Uncle. But it's just got to be done, you know."

They climbed the fence as Bill had done and set off in the direction of the house, which soon came into view through the shrubbery and trees. As they drew nearer, Dorothy saw that Nearma was a large white frame house with green shutters in the conventional New England style. A wide veranda ran along the front of the house and on the far side a massive field-stone chimney broke the expanse of clapboard between the rows of windows. The drive swung round the front of the building and turned sharply to the rear cutting the wide lawn on the near side. The grounds were beautifully landscaped. On a bright summer's day it must indeed be a lovely spot. Just then it looked bleak and drear in the steady autumn downpour.

They reached the drive without sighting Bill, and followed it to the back of the house. Presently Uncle Abe was knocking on the kitchen door.

His second knock was followed by the sound of footsteps and the door opened to disclose an enormously fat negress whose head was bound with a bright red bandanna. The angry glare on her round black face changed to a delighted grin as she recognized her visitor.

"Lord, lordy," she exclaimed. "If it ain't Uncle Abe River hisself. Come in outer de wet. You sure is a sight fer sore eyes. Ain't seen you nohow fer a month er Sundays!"

Liza bustled her callers through an outer pantry into a spacious kitchen.

"I wuz over ter Cross River," said Uncle Abe, seating himself in a proffered chair.

"An' you is allus so good an 'commydatin', Liza, I 'lowed I'd drop in an—"

"Find out whedder Liza would ask you t' dinner," chuckled that good natured person. "Reckon you ain't livin' so high now'days in dat der cabin."

"Yo' sho' is a good guesser," grinned Uncle Abe. "But I likes ter see ol' frien's an' I wanted speshul ter ax if Marse Joyce could gimme a spell o' work rakin' leaves er sump'n."

Liza pursed her lips an shook her head vigorously.

"'Tain't likely dat man'd give you nothin'," she said darkly. "De goin's on hyar lately is sure terrubul. Wat wid all dese strange men in de house an' de young gemmun dey brought in han'cuffed las' night—an' right froo dis hyar kitchen too —I'se jes' 'bout ready ter give notice. But I mustn't say nothin'! Who is dis hyar boy wid you, Uncle?"

Dorothy made a quick decision. "Not a boy, Auntie—a girl," she said quietly. "—And a friend of the young man who was brought here last night."

"Sakes alive!" exploded the stout cook. "Wat's all dis I'm a-hearin'?"

"Yo'all hearin' de spittin' trufe, Liza," chimed in Uncle Abe earnestly. "Miss Do'thy am de qual'ty. Jes' yo' listen ter wat she say."

Dorothy waited for no more comment. With a few deft word strokes she painted a vivid picture of last evening's happenings at the Conway house. Then having aroused a wide-eyed interest in her story, she went on to tell of the adventure in Uncle Abe's cabin and the morning's experiences.

"I am not trying to make trouble between you and Mr. Joyce," she ended, "but if you will help me to free that young gentleman—he must be either George or Terry—you'll be doing a very fine thing and my father will see you come to no harm."

"I'se 'spected fo' some time Marse Joyce wuz er bad man," said Liza, "but I ain't a-skeert of him. Wat you want I should do, Miss Do'thy?"

"I just want you to tell me some things,

Liza. Then you go on getting dinner and I'll see what I can do for my friend."

"Hadn't I better call in Marse Bill?"

"No, not yet. If anything goes wrong in the house I want to have someone on the outside to phone for the police." She turned to Liza. "Do you know where Mr. Joyce and his men are now?"

"Yes, ma'am. Marse Joyce an' most of 'em done gone somewheres in de big car— left de house 'bout 'n hour ago."

"How many are still here?"

"Two o' dose no-count white men is somewhere in de front part of de house. An' let me tell yo'all if dat white trash comes a-bustin' inter my kitchen agin, dey a-gwine ter git a rollin' pin bounced offen dere skulls!"

"If you can't do it, Liza—I will—" added Uncle Abe.

"Ho—how come I can't do it, Abe? You jes' watch dis pickaninny. I'll bust 'em an' bust 'em good!"

Dorothy giggled. Liza's description of herself as a pickaninny had upset her gravity for the moment.

"I can see you're both going to be useful. But tell me, Auntie—do you know where they're keeping this young man?"

"He's in de blue room, Missy. I done tote up his breakfas' to de do'. Marse Joyce give de odder two girls de day off, so I'se cook an' waitress an' chambermaid today. You run along, Miss Do'thy an' if dose cheap ivory rollers try ter git fresh —jes' holler fo' Aunt Liza—she'll bust 'em!"

Dorothy had started for the pantry when Uncle Abe sprang out of his chair and caught her arm.

"'Scuse me, Missy," he apologized then went on eagerly—"I'se got er idee."

"Yes? What is it, Uncle?"

"Dey's logs an' dey's kindlin' in der entry, missy. I done seen 'em when we come in. Well, Miss Do'thy, you tote some kindlin'—an' I'll carry a couple er logs an'—"

"Fine! We'll do it!" Dorothy's alert mind had grasped the plan before Uncle Abe's tongue could give utterance to it.

"An' de bes' part of it is, honey," grinned

Liza, "dat all de rooms on dis flo' has fireplaces an' mos' of dem upstairs too. Marse Joyce, he's a crank on open fires."

Dorothy chuckled. "Lucky break for us." She took a small armful of kindling that Uncle Abe held out to her.

"Yo'all better foller me," said the old darky, "I knows de way 'bout dis house, Miss Do'thy."

He pushed open a swinging door and they slipped into a dining room, panelled in white pine. It was an attractive room and Dorothy decided that despite his criminal traits, John J. Joyce was a man of taste. Uncle Abe tiptoed across the room and paused in the doorway to the hall.

"We better see who's downstairs befo' we goes up," he whispered, and trotted off along the corridor.

He stopped at a closed door near the foot of the staircase and lifted his hand to knock. But before his knuckles had touched the panel, the heavy oak swung inward and they were confronted by the prizefighter whom Dorothy had last seen heating a poker in the Conway house.

"'Scuse us, suh. We'se bringin' wood fo' de fire."

The big man glared at them for a moment. Then apparently satisfied, he stepped aside. "O.K. Thought I heard someone snoopin' around. Dump those logs in the box and then get out."

He paid no more attention to them. Slouching stiffly in a big chair before the fire, he became immediately engrossed in the Sunday paper.

Uncle Abe dropped the logs into the woodbox, and Dorothy knelt on the hearth and piled her kindling beside it. In rising to her feet her head brushed Uncle Abe's arm, knocking off the soft felt hat Bill had loaned her. Quick as a flash she retrieved it and thrust it back on her head.

"A boy with a girl's bob!"

Dorothy turned sharply and found herself staring into the muzzle of an automatic.

"Stand right where you are," barked the big man, as he got up out of his chair. "And you too, dinge—" The revolver swerved for a second in Abe's direction. "Ol' Man

River and the girl, of course—we expected you to show up. The laugh's on you, all right. Where's your boy friend?"

"Right here!" Bill Bolton stepped from behind the heavy window draperies, his revolver trained on the gangster's stomach. "Drop that gun—drop it, or I'll drill you!" Then as the automatic crashed to the floor, a smile spread over his tanned face. "And this time the laugh is on you, my friend," he added softly.

"Oh, *yeah?*" came a rasping voice from the hall doorway. "You drop *your* rod, bo'—and stick 'em up! Don't move— you're covered. Now laugh that one off— ha-ha!"

Bill's gun fell to the floor and his hands rose slowly upwards. In the doorway stood the bald man—the other member that Dorothy had spied on in the library of the Conway house.

Chapter XVI

THE BOOK

The newcomer limped a couple of paces into the room. His left arm and one leg were swathed in bandages.

"What price rock salt?" remarked Bill pleasantly, still reaching toward the ceiling.

Despite her qualms, Dorothy could not help smiling. The bald man's face became scarlet with fury.

"Another crack like that and I'll give you a taste of something harder than rock salt," he roared. "And when I get through with him that guy who was so free with his shotgun last night will wish he'd never been born!"

Bill ignored this outburst. "That gat was my only weapon," he announced without rancor. "This house is in New York State, so if you want to burn in Sing Sing, shoot—I'm tired of holding up my arms."

He lowered his hands and thrust them into his trousers pockets.

The bald man looked daggers but he did not pull the trigger. Instead he turned on his partner.

"Why don't you do something, Chick?" he growled. "You know I'm laid up— oughta be in bed right now, for that matter."

"Say, Eddie," complained the burly fellow, "I'm stiff as a board myself—I got peppered all down my back and you know it."

"Aw, quit yer grousin'. You can still move around. Tie 'em up and we'll dump 'em somewhere till the boss gets back."

"Yeah? An' what do we use fer rope?"

Eddie scratched his head with the butt of his revolver and hobbled over to an armchair. "Stick that gat in yer pocket, Chick," he ordered as he lowered himself carefully into the deep cushions. "I've got 'em covered. Beat it into the kitchen— that fat dinge in there's got plenty of clothesline. Help yerself and tell her I'll come in an' bump her off, if she gets nasty!"

Chick pocketed his revolver and started to walk stiffly across the room when Liza's ample figure appeared in the doorway. In her hands she bore a wooden mixing bowl, brimming with cake batter. The whites of her eyes gleamed dangerously, as she glared at Chick; then she waddled into the room and halted just behind Eddie's chair.

"I done heard what yo'all said jes' now, bald man—" She shook her head slowly from side to side and stared down at the gangster's hairless pate. "Seems ter me you was talkin' 'bout bumpin' some-buddy!"

With his gun covering the three prisoners, Eddie was unable to look up at her. Chick undoubtedly hailed Liza's appearance as relief from the painful necessity of a walk to the kitchen. He sat down on the edge of a chair opposite Eddie and scowled at her sourly. Eddie took up the conversation with the angry woman behind him.

"That's right, nigger," he chuckled hoarsely. "We want some clothesline, to tie up these here nuisances—an' if you don't cough some up right now—I'll bump you off, see?"

"Reckon you got your names mixed—" Without warning Liza brought the solid mixing bowl down upon his unprotected skull.

Eddie collapsed beneath the forceful blow and as he crumpled to the floor, Liza flung the bowl and its contents in Chick's face. Then with an agility surprising in one so cumbersomely made, she catapulted herself at the astonished ruffian. Over went his chair and they crashed in a tangled heap of broken furniture, waving legs and cake batter.

Bill broke into a roar of laughter, but Dorothy wasted no time in being amused at this spectacle. She dove for Bill's gun which Eddie had not bothered to retrieve. She ran over the struggling pair on the floor and held the muzzle to Chick's head.

"Stop fighting!" she commanded. "Stop it at once—"

Chick sat up and tried to scrape the batter out of his eyes. "I ain't fightin'," he growled, "I'm half blind and I'm fair smothered. An' if me back ain't broke it oughter be! Take that Mack truck offen my legs—I can't move, much less put up a scrap!"

"Get up, Liza!" Dorothy had to smile at the fellow's plight. With Bill's help she got the stout negress planted on her feet again. Uncle Abe stood guard with a poker over Eddie. That glum gentleman was heralding his return to consciousness with the most remarkable series of coughing grunts.

"This sure is the craziest rough house I ever got mixed up in," laughed Bill. "Old Baldy over there sounds like a French pig rooting for truffles—"

Dorothy grinned absent-mindedly, her thoughts on the next move to be made.

"We'll let dese two pigs burrer an' grunt down cellar," declared Liza, straightening her turban and smoothing down her apron. "Dere's a empty storeroom down dere—it's got a strong door an' a good bolt, too. Gimme a gun, please Miss Dor'thy. Me an' Uncle Abe can 'tend ter dis white trash."

The negress walked over to Eddie, who stared about the room, a dazed expression on his face.

"Git up an' come along."

Then as Eddie continued to look at her vacantly, she picked him up as if he were a baby and draped him over her broad shoulders.

"Yo'all go first, Liza," said Uncle Abe. He prodded Chick with the gun he had taken from her. "Him an' me'll be right behin'."

Dorothy and Bill watched the odd procession pass from the room.

"Whew!" she exclaimed. "That was a hectic five minutes. But how did you happen to be in here?"

"Got tired of sticking round outside, so slipped in by that window. Eddie was asleep at the time, but he woke up right afterward. Then you and Uncle Abe walked in—and you know the rest. Say, it must be Terry these guys nabbed. Wonder what's become of Stoker and Betty?"

"Heaven only knows," said Dorothy

wearily. "I'll go up and let Terry out and I think the best thing you can do is to phone the state police. With Terry here, we've got enough on Mr. John J. Joyce to hold him, now."

"We sure have. Wonder what the J in John J. Joyce stands for?"

"Well, it will stand for Jay, Jonah and Jinx all in one, *if* you get the police here before he comes back and sets his men free. By the way, I may be going coo-coo with all this, but it seems to me that I keep hearing shots every now and then. There's another—hear it?"

"Somebody's probably potting bunnies in the woods." Bill seemed unconcerned. "I noticed it just after I got in here. Beat it upstairs now, and I'll hunt up a telephone."

Dorothy found the room where Terry was held prisoner by the simple expedient of opening each door as she came to it. The fourth door was locked, but the key was on the outside. It was no surprise to her, upon opening it, to see her friend lying on the bed. A quick glance showed

Dorothy that both windows were barred.

Terry sprang up with a glad cry. "It's sure good to see *you!*" He gave her a good-natured hug. "How in the world did you manage this?"

Dorothy told him as briefly as possible. "What I want to know," she said in conclusion, "is how they happened to catch you napping—and what's become of George Conway and Betty?"

"They didn't catch me napping," Terry retorted. "You and Bill had been gone about an hour and I expected Stoker back from taking Betty home any minute. A Ford drove into the garage, there was a bang on the door and a voice sang out—'Let me in. It's George.' Well, I opened up and—"

"It wasn't George—" supplied Dorothy, as usual going straight to the point. "Joyce and his men nabbed you, of course. That's plain enough. But where are Betty and George?"

"Search me."

Bill burst into the room and stood breathless before them.

"Did you get the police?" asked Dorothy.

"Got headquarters all right. But what do you think's happened?"

"Spill it, Bill. This is no guessing bee," said Terry.

"The sergeant told me they'd had a phone call from Lewis. The old man was frantic. Joyce and his gang were trying to break into his house. The whole caboodle from headquarters are up there now, rounding up John J. Joyce and Company."

"That accounts for the shots we heard," cried Dorothy. "Get on your rubbers, Terry. We're going to hike over to Mr. Lewis's place right now. I want to be in at the finish."

"And I," added Bill, "want to find out what this mess is about!"

They raced downstairs and stopping only long enough to tell Liza and Uncle Abe of this new development, set off for the Lewis property adjoining.

Following hasty directions given them by the darkies, they hurried along a path which led them to a gate in a high wall. The gate was not locked and they continued along the path which crossed the Lewis estate. Presently the dim shape of a large white house appeared through the mist.

"Halt!" A gruff voice arrested them as they were about to ascend the steps at the side entrance. A state trooper barred their way. "Who are you—and what do you want?"

"We are friends of Mr. Lewis," said Dorothy. She explained the circumstances of their arrival.

"Well, we've just sent Joyce and his men to the lockup. The whole crew of 'em. We corralled 'em proper. They'd busted into the house, you know, and it sure would have been a mixup if this fly cop that horned in on the Joyce bunch hadn't clapped his gat to Joyce's head and held up their game until we got here."

"Oh, that must have been Michael Michaels—the private inquiry agent who came to Uncle Abe's last night," said Bill. "We'd like to go in the house, officer."

"O. K. with me. There's some kind of a pow-wow goin' on in the living room. I'll take you in there."

He opened the door and led them across the square hall into the living room. Here they found a surprise awaiting them.

"Betty! George!" cried Dorothy. She flew across the room to her friend. "I'm so glad you're safe. How did you get here?"

"Oh, darling! It's too exciting for words!" gurgled Betty as they hugged each other. "And George was so brave—he—"

"Mr. Lewis and his chauffeur stopped our Lizzie last night," broke in Stoker. "Told us Joyce and his men were likely to hold us up down the road. So we left the Ford and came over here with Mr. Lewis. And we've been here ever since."

"Listen, George!" said that old gentleman, and both girls giggled. "Hadn't you better introduce your friends? This young lady in overalls is Miss Dixon, I take it?"

"She certainly is," smiled Stoker and performed the necessary introductions.

The other men in the room proved to be Michael Michaels and an inspector of the state police. For a few minutes everybody seemed to be talking at once. Bill told George and Mr. Lewis of his adventures with Dorothy, while Terry explained his capture by the Joyce gang to the inspector and Michaels.

"Listen!" said Dorothy and threw a reproving glance at the others' unsuppressed smiles—"Will somebody please tell me what Mr. Joyce has been trying to steal from Stoker?"

"Why, that's so," interjected Mr. Lewis, "you have no idea, of course—"

"No, except that it's probably mixed up with that book, *Aircraft Power Plants,* I think it's called—"

The old gentleman looked at her in unfeigned astonishment. "Listen, Michaels!" he cried. "She says this business is connected with that book. Pretty good guess, eh?"

"Certainly is," returned the detective. "But the book is a mystery in itself, and one we haven't yet solved."

"But what *was* Joyce after?" interrupted Bill with a show of impatience.

"The plans, of course," said Stoker Conway.

"But what plans?"

"The plans of my father's new aircraft engine. I knew nothing about it until Mr. Lewis told me last night."

"Where are the plans, and what has the book to do with them?" broke in Dorothy.

"Listen, young lady," began Mr. Lewis, when Michaels the detective stopped him with a gesture.

"Better let me tell them, sir," he suggested. "These young people have a right to know."

The old gentleman nodded approval and the detective, after biting off the end of a cigar, continued to talk while the others grouped about him. "About two weeks ago," he said, "Mr. Lewis called at my New York office. There he told me the following story. Six weeks before his death, Mr. Conway came over here and told Mr. Lewis that he had perfected plans for an aircraft motor which would develop very high power on a very small consumption of gasoline."

"That's just what all the inventors are after now," interposed Bill.

"Why, I should say so!" cried Dorothy. "If *Wispy's* motor didn't lap up the gas like a thirsty camel, I'd never have been forced to land in that woodlot yesterday afternoon!"

"All very interesting, I'm sure—" Terry's voice was sarcastic. "But do let's hear what Mr. Michaels is trying to tell us!"

"That's all right," smiled the detective. "Let's see—where was I? Oh, yes, the motor: well, the inventor told Mr. Lewis that his partner and sales agent had ruined him financially, and that now he was convinced that he'd been swindled, and that Joyce was a crook. Mr. Lewis suggested Mr. Conway take the matter to the courts, and offered to advance money for legal expenses. Mr. Conway said he hadn't sufficient evidence for a case; that Joyce had covered his tracks too well. Then he spoke about the plans for this new motor he'd just completed. He said that Joyce knew about it and was trying to get control of the thing; but that outside of stealing the plans outright, Joyce could do nothing, as the partnership had been dissolved. And at the same time he told Mr. Lewis that he knew he was suffering from an incurable disease and could live but a few months longer at most."

"Listen, Michaels—let me tell it," interrupted old Lewis. "You are wandering all over the place . . . Your father, George, said that should he have the new motor built, Joyce would undoubtedly make trouble, and he, Conway, wanted to die in peace. He told me he was going to entrust me with the plans and would send them to me after he had made some slight changes in them. And he said that he would send me his check to cover the expense of building and exploiting the engine. 'After I'm gone, you attend to it for George,' he said. 'That boy has no mechanical ability, and he's too young to market a thing like this motor. Joyce or other wolves like him would rob him of it in twenty four hours.' And that, was the last time I saw John Conway alive."

The old gentleman pulled out a handkerchief and blew his nose violently. "He wouldn't see me when I called, nor would he mention the plans over the phone. He died while I was in Boston on business. When I got back the next day, I found a package from him waiting for me. Of course, I thought it would contain the plans and his check. When I opened it up I found nothing but a book—*Aircraft Power Plants,* by a man named Jones. I was naturally surprised, and searched its pages from cover to cover, but found no papers of any kind. I've even read every word of it since then. And its pages have been tested for invisible ink. But I've had my trouble and pains for nothing."

"I wonder why Father didn't tell me of those plans?" George remarked rather wistfully.

"That I can't explain, my boy. As you know now, I thought you had them. Either that you had removed them from the book before it left your house, or that your father had changed his mind and given them to you. Anyway, I decided to await developments. Nothing happened until Joyce, who had been in Europe since Conway's death, returned home a couple of weeks ago. He came to see me and asked me outright if I knew anything about Conway's airplane motor plans. I never liked nor trusted Joyce, but I saw no harm in telling him the truth. For of course I figured that George must have set the wheels in motion for the sale of the motor long before. Joyce could do nothing about it at this late date."

"But to my astonishment, the man told me the motor had not been marketed—that he would have heard if any company had bought it. 'Either that boy's got the plans,' he said, 'or Conway had two copies of the book and sent you the wrong one—' I didn't understand how the book came into it and told him so. 'Conway always sent important papers through the mail by placing them between the pages of a book,' he assured me. 'Thought they would travel safer that way.'

"Well, he changed the subject then, and left. I got nervous about what I'd told him, and hired Michaels to watch the fellow. Michaels dug up a lot of things about Joyce, and managed to get himself placed on his staff of roughnecks. If he could have been in two places at once, all this trouble over at the Conway house last night would never have come off."

Dorothy spoke from her place on the couch beside Betty. "How did you happen to go there last night?"

"I wanted to find out if George really had another copy of the book. Later I learned from Michaels that Joyce's men had tried to torture the boy into telling them where the plans were—and that then he intended to kidnap him. I was on my way over there to warn him when we met on the road. He wanted to put young Walters wise, but I was sure the Joyce gang wouldn't hurt his friend. I had promised Michaels not to go ahead on my own hook until I saw him. Perhaps I was wrong, but I did what I thought was best for George's interests. I've heard since that they just about tore the house apart, looking for the other copy of that book!"

"Do you happen to have the copy that was sent you, here in the house?" asked Dorothy.

"Yes—right here, on the table." Michaels handed it to her.

Dorothy pored over the book for a few minutes, then laid it down. "Mr. Lewis, do you mind if I take it home with me?"

"Why, of course not—keep it as long as you wish."

"Thanks," she smiled. "Now, you gentlemen want to plan about what to do with Joyce and Co., and Bill and I have some gas to buy and a plane to fly home. So I'll say *au revoir* for the present!"

Chapter XVII

THE TEST

On a morning some three months later, the private flying field on the Bolton place was the mecca of a considerable portion of New Canaan's population. The ridge road and the surrounding meadows were jammed with cars that flaunted license plates of a dozen different states. Although the December sun shone brightly in a cobalt sky, the crowd shivered and stamped on the frozen ground for the winter air was icy. All eyes were turned upward toward an airplane, high above their heads, which swept the sky in immense, horizontal circles.

A small group of people bundled in heavy fur coats stood and chatted by the open doors of the hangar.

"I almost wish they'd come down," said George Conway. "They must be half-dead for want of sleep, and they've already beaten the world's record by hours.　It must be a terrific strain, especially for Dorothy."

"Oh," cried Betty Mayo. "Isn't she marvelous?—and Bill, too!"

"They're a pair of young idiots!" growled old Mr. Lewis, whose false teeth were chattering. "But I must admit they're first class sportsmen to stay up all this time for a friend!"

"You said it," declared Terry Walters, and glanced at his wrist watch. "In exactly one minute, they'll have been up one hundred and one hours, without refueling. Gosh, it's wonderful!　That motor of your father's is some humdinger, Stoker!"

"Why, it's simply adorable!"　Betty was brimming over with excitement.　"And I just can't help being glad that that horrid Mr. Joyce and his men are being sent to Sing Sing for years and years and years! It's too—"

"Here they come!"　The crowd yelled and roared and swarmed toward the roped-off enclosure.

Sure enough—At last the big plane was

spiralling downward. It landed lightly on the frozen ground and bowled across the field. The crowd surged in, but there was no sign of life, no movement about the plane. Mechanics jerked open the door, and there, side by side, grimy, worn, unkempt, were Dorothy Dixon and Bill Bolton, sleeping like children!

Somehow they were taken into the Bolton's house and put to bed, where they continued to sleep for twelve hours, while certain anxious gentlemen waited about, impatiently demanding interviews.

The pair eventually looked up from quantities of ham and eggs in the dining room, to greet their visitors.

"Now, I want to talk business," said the portly man who led the van. "Mr. Conway will not discuss the matter. He refers me to you—"

"Oh, you can talk to her," said Bill. He motioned to Dorothy. "She's run this show from start to finish."

"And what," asked the portly gentleman, coming at once to the point, "will you take for that motor, Miss Dixon?"

"Hmmm—A hundred hours, without refueling," remarked Dorothy, thoughtfully buttering a slice of toast. "I hope you've given that some thought."

"I have given it several thoughts. Name a price."

"A million," said Dorothy.

"Dollars?"

Bill kicked her under the table.

"Pounds, certainly," said Dorothy. "I went to England last year, and after I learned how to figure their complicated money, I've never been able to unlearn it!"

She smiled benignly upon the company.

Bill nodded. "Dorothy's some little bargainer, ain't she?" he said delightedly, with his mouth full.

"Give you a million dollars," said the portly gentleman.

"Give up your place," said Dorothy, "and let some of these other gentlemen into the game."

"A million and a half," said the portly gentleman, edging closer to the table.

"Make it two million and you win."

"Done!"

"Thank you," smiled Dorothy. "Now please make the check payable to George Conway."

The gentlemen filed out of the room.

"Gee, you're a whizbang, Dorothy!" Bill exploded as soon as they were alone. "Some Christmas present for Stoker!"

"You're not so bad yourself," laughed the girl. "That kick of yours was worth just a million dollars!"

Five minutes later, the kitchen door of the Bolton's house was flung open and a black face crowned with an aureole of woolly hair peered in. "Has yo'all heard de news, Liza?" panted Uncle Abe in great excitement.

"G'wan home, niggah, I'ze busy makin' waffle fo' de chilluns," retorted the Bolton's cook. "Golly, but dey sure is hungry!"

"Miss Dorothy done sol' dat motah fo' two million dollars. I wuz stickin' roun' outside an' done hear de gen'men talkin' 'bout it."

"Lan's sakes, but dat a pile er money,"

said Liza pouring batter on to the hot waffle iron. "How come Marse Bill was able ter build dat engin'? I thought dat de plans was lost?"

"You sho' has a one-track mind, Liza," Uncle Abe observed contemptuously. "And dat track spells nuthin' but kitchen. My young Missy *found* dem plans! She beat all dose big detecatives to it!"

"Do tell! Whar was dey?"

"In er book, Liza."

"Shucks, I done heard 'bout de book. Dey warn't no plans inside it."

"Huh! Dey sho wuz, too!"

"Whar dey at?"

"Miss Dor'thy done took er knife an' ripped dat book erpart! Dat little lady is de quality, an' she sure am smart. De plans was on thin paper, pasted in de back whar de leaves o' de book am sewed togedder."

"Do tell!" Liza shook her head. "But what I nevah did un'erstan' wuz why Marse Joyce tried ter kidnap de other boys and girls."

"Liza, you sho' is dumb. It all come

out in de trial. Firs' Marse Joyce think Marse George know 'bout de plans, so his men try ter make him tell. Den when Miss Dor'thy busted up dat party, he know dat de other chilluns would sho' crab his game if dey wuz let loose ter tell 'bout it."

"Abe, you is crazy! How dat man goin' ter keep all dose young folks locked in his house while he try to sell dem plans? De police sure find dem befo' he's able ter do dat!"

"No. Liza, you's wrong agin. Marse Joyce knew a lot about dem plans. Marse Conway had done tol' him consider'ble about dem, and Marse Joyce done tell de Rooshians what Marse Conway tell him. De Rooshians say dey give him a heap of money jes' as soon as he build dat engine."

"An' Marse Joyce figured he'd beat it to Rooshia jes' as soon as he could put his han's on de plans?" said Liza.

"Dat's right—" nodded the old darky. "You ain't quite ez dumb ez yo' looks, niggah. An' de way Marse George is a-hangin' roun' Miss Betty—"

"Yo'all talks too much," Liza cut him short. "Lan' sakes! Gossipin' at yo' age! Tote dis hyar plate of hot waffles inter der dinin' room. De young folks am hungry!"

THE END

Dorothy's further adventures will be found in the fourth book of this series, *Dorothy Dixon and the Double Cousin.*